Mr. Hendriks

Statistics of Indian Revenue and Taxation

SALZWASSER
VERLAG

Mr. Hendriks

Statistics of Indian Revenue and Taxation

Reprint of the original, first published in 1859.

1st Edition 2022 | ISBN: 978-3-37512-722-0

Verlag (Publisher): Salzwasser Verlag GmbH, Zeilweg 44, 60439 Frankfurt, Deutschland
Vertretungsberechtigt (Authorized to represent): E. Roepke, Zeilweg 44, 60439 Frankfurt, Deutschland
Druck (Print): Books on Demand GmbH, In de Tarpen 42, 22848 Norderstedt, Deutschland

STATISTICS

OF

INDIAN REVENUE

AND

TAXATION.

PROOF COPY OF PAPER READ

TO THE

STATISTICAL SOCIETY OF LONDON,

18th May, 1858,

BY

MR. HENDRIKS.

LONDON:

PRINTED BY HARRISON AND SONS, ST. MARTIN'S LANE, W.C.

1858.

On the Statistics   REVENUE *ani* TAXITION.
- By PEEDEBICK HENDEIKS.

. [Read before the Statistical Society, 18th May, 1858.]

CONTENTS:

Introductory Remarks.

INDLAN REVENUE STATISTICS have usually been regarded as anything but an*attractive subject of study. The causes which, until a v^y recent period, induced an apathetic distaste to the discussion of details of any branch of Indian administration, told with, if ·possible, greater force, when the Revenue or system of Taxation was in question. The intricacies of Land Tenures, the controversies they had given rise to, and the somewhat too profuse employment of Indian legal and fiscal terms worded in difierent vernaculars, contributed in no mean degree to this result.

The rapid march of the great and stirring events of which India has lately been, and still is, the theatre—the example which the East India Company, and those oflicially connected with India in Parliament have vied with each other in enforcing on the public, as to the urgent need of a more popular and a wider spread study of the

A2

elements of Indian finance—all justify an impression, that efforts to simplify and explain the special nature of those elements will not be looked upon with as much indifference as was formerly their fate.

These observations must be understood as made in a general sense, the Statistical Society having uniformly proved, for the last twenty years or more, that it did not share in the prevalent unconcern on Indian topics.

A full consideration of the leading branches of Indian Revenue, from a British point of view, appears to divide itself as follows, into distinct, but at the same time intimately connected, heads of enquiry, respecting :—

(1). The present condition of the Indian Revenue; the pressure of Taxation, and the territorial area and extent of population from which it is raised.

(2). The productive, financial, and industrial condition of India; and the degree in which experience and facts have shown it to be susceptible of improvement through the promotion of agriculture and public works; better means of irrigation and transit by canals and railways; and an amended system of Land Settlement.

(3). The fiscal conditions that regulate Indian finance, compared with those applicable to British finance.

(4). The facts and Statistics bearing upon the past history and progress of Revenue and Taxation in British India, during the Sixty-Four Years 1792-3 to 1855-6.

The risks of too broad a generalization upon data really applicable only to a limited portion of surface, are both numerous and perplexing, and, unless extreme care be used, may lead to mistaken deductions upon many of the branches comprised in the Revenue administration of so vast an empire, including territory nearly seven times as extensive, and population nearly five times as numerous, as Great Britain. It must also be kept in recollection how widely the distinct nations comprised in this empire differ in origin, temperament, language, and industry, and in their respective advance in civilization; and what various influences they are subject to, of climate, soil, hereditary custom, and caste.

Civilians who have had the advantage of practical experience in the service of the East India Company abroad, are not necessarily more free from the entanglement of such causes of error, than the enquirer at home. They are frequently imbued with views on Indian administrative points, correct enough so far as relates to the particular localities of one Presidency, but by no means deserving that character when applied to the formation of a judgment upon the circumstances of other Presidencies. Of the latter they may not, perhaps, possess any local knowledge whatever. The races of people, their agricultural, industrial, and social condition may be quite difforent from those of the inhabitants of the part of India where the official life of these civilians has been spent.

On the other hand, in England, we are chiefly dependent on the information and instruction upon Indian topics derivable from documentary evidence of facts and figures. These are not to be found in excess, in a published form. Bather the contrary ; and there is cer- .tainly wanting a condensed Beport, for each Presidency, upon the same order and classes of statistical facts, illustrative of their agriculture, trade, manufactures, prices, markets, means of communication, and rates of wages for skilled and for general labour. The differences in the social, family, and conjugal, condition of the people; and last, but not least, a sufficiently near approximate estimate of their wealth, in real and personal property, all deserve and demand investigation. It may be true that to set on foot, and carry out, such an inquiry and report, would be an expensive and laborious undertaking ; but there is reason to infer that it would repay itself a thousandfold, ^nd contribute to the material prosperity, and through that to the moral well-being, of the population of India, to an extent which even the sanguine would not be found to have over estimated.

Proceeding with our outline of the subject before us, and promising that the utmost it will be endeavoured to accomplish is to lay down some general principles on which it may be discussed by thia Society; we have at the outset to confine our attention to the first topic of inquiry that has been alluded to, Wz.:—

I.—*The present condition of the Indian Revenue, the pressure of Taxation, and the territorial area and extent of population from which it is raised.*

The latest period for which complete accounts have been received and publis^^ by the East India House, are for the year ended 30th April, 1850. The position of the various branches of Revenue sicfce tlijp.t date is not supposed to have materially altered, and no serious qrror will ensue from 'viewing the Revenue for the financial year **1855-50, as about representing its present position.

In Indian Accounts the difl'erent rates of exchange for the Eupee cause some apparent discrepancy in the separate returns of total income and expenditure, and of surplus or deficiency.

The basis of the following first TABLE A, is the Pari. Bet. (lO/'S?). In this Eeturn, as in the one of which it is a continuation (336/'55), the Items are reduced to Sterling, at the rate of *2s.* per Bupee, throughout, so that the conversion can be brought from one denomination to the other by the rules of decimal notation.

For clearness of reading this, and the other tables which follow, as well as for convenience of printing, it has been found expedient to discard the units, tens, and hundreds, and to express each Item in Millions and Thousands of Pounds only, so that three ciphers, 000, are to be added at the right hand of each Sum.*

TABLE A.

TOTAL REVENUE *derived from, all sources, in each* PRESIDENCY *and in the whole* 0/BRITISH INDIA, *in One Year,* 1855-56.

1	3	s	4	5	6	7
Separate Branches of Revenue.	Bengal.	No'.'Wstn. Provinces.	Presidency. r Madras, (?	Bombay,	Punjab.	Whole of Britisii India,
	Mlns, £	Mlns, # £	^llus. £	Mlns.. £ .	Mins. £	Mlns. £
1. Land Revenue.........	4-668	5-000	3-642	2-846	0-954	
2. Sayer Revenue (or. Sundry Items of] mixed direct andf indirect Taxation)J	0.499 '	0-303	0-247	0-116	0-079	••»44
3. Excise ....|.........	0-045					0'045
4. Moturjiha (or Pro-i perty and Incomet Tax, recently dis-1 continued)...............J			0-109			0'109
ft. Salt Tax	1-082	0-549	0-541	0-275	0-204	i-651
6. Opium Revenue	4-172			1-024		5-196
7, Post Office	' 0-045	0-087	0-059	0-022	0-024	0'237
8. Stamp Duties	0-223	0-169	0-071	0-069	0-020	0'552
0. CufltomR	1-541	0-078	0-140	0-348		" i'loy
10, Mint Duties............	0-119		0-019	0-058		0-196
11. Miscellaneous (in-l eluding Tribute l from Nativestates,} Pilotage, Toll, and l Ferry Dues)........j	0-625	0-074	0-459	0195	0017	1'^70
Total Gross Revenue	13-019	6-260	5-287	4-953	1-298	30-817
Total Gross Charges	13-768	2-533	5-537	5-123	1-411	28-372
Net Indian Surplus.........		3-727				2'445
Net IndiairDefiefenEy.. ,	0-749	....	0-250	0-170	0-113	

    * *An* examples^ in col. 2 of the annexed TABLE A, it will be found that the Land Kctriiiic for licngal was (in the year 1855-56) 4'668 Mlns.   In other words, it was 4,668,000/., the exact figures of the account being 4,668,156. .lgain, in col. 6, under the head of Stamp Duties, the receipts in the Punjab are given at 0'02(| Mlns. £; meaning 20,0^0/., the precise figures of the original account making them 20,1671.

item of this TABLE A will he more fully referred to in the fourth, or last, part of this paper; in which a brief account will be given of the progress of the separate branches of Revenue during the Sixty-Four years 1792-3 to 11855-56, with calculated annual averages for each five years. At the present first step in our inquiry it win be well not to encumber it with too many figures. What we want at the outset is an approximate and condensed view of the amount of Revenue and its distribution over tlie several great divisions of India; without refereiice to any consideration of what part of such Revenue is Taxatiompressing upon the people, and of what part is Government Income', the pressure of which does not fall upon them. This will be presently discussed. In the meanwhile let us restrict ourselve^ to observing that if we recapitulate from TABLE A the Items of Gross Revenue from the several Presidencies, viz.;—

	£
1. Bengal	13,019,000
2. North-West Provinces	6,260,000
3. Madras	5,287,000
4. Bombay	4,953,000
5. Punjab	1,2'J8,OO0

we arrive at a total for India of 30,817,0001. of Gross Revenue.

A line has been added to this, and to the other Tables, showing the Gross Charges, another showing the Indian Surplus or Deficiency. This is to be understood as irrespective of tlffe receipts and disbursements of the Homo Treasury for it3 establishments and liabilities in England. " *

With these explanations, we may now revert to the figures of TABLE A. And the immediate question of most importance, on the face of those figures, is the ascertainment of the proportion which each source of Revenue bears to the total raised. The per centage calculation^,, are contained in the next TABLE B; and, under, the fourth head of our inquiry, will be found Tables for which the Per C.mtage proportions have been similarly computed for the several quinquennial periods from 1792-3 to 1855-6. These will be useful for reference, and will show, far better than undigested figures, the fiuctuations between those dates. We have, however, at the moment, to restrict our attention more particularly to TABLE B.

It wUl be observed how wide a range of difference exists in the proportions of the several sources of Revenue. For instance, the Land-Tax (so called) contributes less than 36 Per Cent, of the total Revenue in Bengal, and in the North-West Provinces nearly 80 Per Cent., whilst the average for India is about yy-J per Cent. The Salt-Tax is nearly 16 Per Cent, of the total Revenue in the Punjab, whilst in Bombay it contributes only 5^ per Cent, of its Revenue, the average for India approaching 8| per Cent. Next the Optiw#

Revenue, does not exist at all in the North-West Provinces, Madras, or the Punjab, but covers 32 Per Cent,, or not far short of -jrd/of the Bengal Revenue, and 21 per Cent., or more than -j-th of the Bombay Revenue, and quite ^th of the whole Indian Revenue. Then the *Customs* which are under 7 Per Cent., or less than xjth of the Indian Revenue, do not contribute anything to the Punjab Revenue, only make up 1| per Cent, of the North-West Provinces Revenue, and at their maximum in Bengal are under 12 per cent. The last of the larger Items is the *DUseeUaneoas Revenue,* including Tributes from native states, &c., and it averages   per'Cent, for India, is not much more than 1 Per Cent, in the North-West Provinces, but reaches 8| per Cent, in Madras.

TABLE B.

PER CENTAQES *of the* REVENUE FROM EACH SOURCE *to the Total Revenue raised, in each Presidency of* INDIA; *in the Tear* 1855-56, (calculated from TABLE A.)

1 Separate Sources of , . Revenue.	2 Bengal.	S No.*-WgtD. Provinces.	4 Madras.	'6 Bombay.	S Punjab.	7 Wbolo of British India.
	Per Cent.	Per Cent.	Per Cent.	Per Cent.	Per Cent.	Per Cent.
1.-Land....................	35-85	79*87	68-91	67-45	73-50	55-62
2. Sayer (For- ex-l planation. see? Table A)	o3-83	4-84	4-67	2-34	6-00	4-0+
3. Excise	•35			....		•>5
4. Moturpha (Fori explanaUon> see^ Table A)		...»	2-06	....		•35
5. Salt	8-31	S-JI	10-24	5-55		8-6o
6. Opium	3204			20-67	....	i6-86
7. Post Office	•35	1-39	1-12	-45	1-85	•77'
8. Stamp Duties	1-72	2-70	1*34	1-40	1-54	f79
9. Customs	11-84	1-25	2-63	7-03		6-83
10. Mint DuUes.............	•91		-35	1-17	«	•64
ir. Miscellaneous (Foil explanation, see? Table A) ....ij	4-80	118	8-68	3-94	1-31	4'45
Total Revenue	100*	100*	100*	100*	ICO*	100'

Statistical calculatious of the *pressure of Taxation* on each head of the population, and on each square mile of territory, in certain parts of India, were recently (Feb. 1858) submitted to Parliament. (See Keturn 86, of 1858). The object was to enable comparison with the relative weight, as measured in money, of the incidence of Taxation in the United Kingdom. The figures given of the pressure on each inhabitant of the North-Western Provinces (Regulation and Non-Regulation) are 3s.   and on each inhabitant of the Bombay Presidency Ss. 92J. The first of these results is based upon the ratio to the number of inhabitants, of the aggregate of six items, viz.: Laud Revenue, "Ibkaree or Spirit licenses, Stamps, Miscellaneous Revenue, Saye? Revenue (a technical term signifying items of direct and indirect taxation not included in miscellaneous revenue), and Customs Duties. The other result is based on two items only, viz.: Land aSid Sayer Revenues.

But the question at once arises, if, in either of these examples, the first and largest item, of Land Revenue, or so called Land-Tax, should be included in the estimate ?

This amounts to an inquiry, whether Land in India is taxed at all.

It may readily be admitted that whenever and wherever—under Hindoo or Mussulman despotism, or under British rule—the Land Revenue, paid to the government out of the produce of the soil, in money or in kind, exceeded a fair amount of Rent, the excess beybnd that normal or natural rent, was, practically as well as nominally, a Tax. But, if we admit thia argument, we must reject that imdue extension of its premiss which would include the normal rent, or any amount less than the nUrmdl rent, in the designation of a tax.

The archaeology of the Muhammedan *Khwrauj,* or Land-Tax, is by no means so abstruse or uninviting as to repel an inquirer of ordinary patience. It rests upon foundations which have nothing of the questionableness or mythical speculation ,of the Hindoo law. We may hq^e restrict ourselves to observing that there is ample evidence in favour of the conclusion that, in its origin, and in the theory of its incidence, for centuries upon centuries, the Land Revenue of India was a Rent and not a tax. We shall have to recur to this hereafter.

But it was a Rent in a form all modem political economy has declared to be the worst in which it can be assessed. It was a given portion of the gross produce; such as the greed of the rulers, or the abject state of the ruled, was fain or forced to let grow into the liou's share. Theoretically, even at its origin, it was a species of Rent; but there ensued, too often, a surplus exaction, which was a Tax. This has, however, been changed; and, in recent times, years in British India may be counted as centuries, if we consider the great revoliitiouS they have made in the laws, customs, traditions, and prejudices of races erroneously supposed to be imbued with an

inflexible immutability.   In nothing has this been more obvious,
than in th.e large reforms of the principles of Land Eevenue collection.   And, if the British sway in India had not nobler records, it
might well be proud that in this most important matter it has swept
away the inherited injustice of former ages.

Living, present history will prove this.   We may with advantage
be instructed respecting it by a passage to be- found in the last of
the remarkable series of state papers recently issued by the East
India Company.   The Land Revenue'"system, in its latest form of
improvement, is there criticized in words proclaiming that no oppression on the Landholder can have substantial existence any longer—
words which, if inserted in a general code of administration, might
be deserving of the designation of the Indian Magna Charta.   The
" Memorandum of Improvements in the Administration of India,
Feb. 1858 "—the paper here referred to—seems founded in chief'
measure upon an application, to the peculiar circumstances of India,
of the rationale common to all state Land Eevenues, or so called
Land-Taxes, 'which have originated in the form of reserved rents.
The characteristics of the different Tenures of Land in the several
Presidencies Are described at some length in the Memorandum, and
in continuation of what bad been previously officially stated in the
special Eetum of June 1857 (Pari. Paper 112, Sess. 2).   Statisti-
cally an exception must be taken to the estimate of the proportion
of Eevenue derived from the Land, as being Two-Thirds.   It would
be more correct to feay (as already shown) that the proportion is
above One-Half, or about 55| Per Cent.

The part of the Memorandum it is now proposed to quote in
full, runs thus (see pages 7-8) :—

"Nearly two-thirds of the revenue of India consist of the rent of land.   So far
as this resource extends in any country, the public nece^ities of the country may be ,
said to be provided for, at no expense to the people at large.   'Wbae • the original
right of the state to the land of the country has been reserved, and its natural, but
no more than its natural, rents made available to meet the public expenditure, '.he
people may be said to be so far untaxed j because the Governngent only takes from
them as a tax what they would otherwise have paid as a rent to a private landlord.
This proposition undoubtedly requires modification in the case of a Ryot or peasant
cultivating his own land ; but even in his case, if the Government demand does not
exceed the amount which the land could pay as rent if let to a solvent tenant (that
is, the price of fts peculiar advantages of fertility or situation), the Government
only reserves ta itself, instead of conceding to the cultivator, the profit of a kind of
natural monopoly, Ijeaving to him the same reward of his labour and capital which
is obtained by the remainder of the industrious population.   Any amount whatever
of revenue, therefore, derived from the rent of land, cannot be regarded, generally
speaking, ns a burtien on the tax-paying community.   But to this it is of course
essential that ths dekiand of revenue should be kept within the limits of a fair rent.

Under the Native Governments, and in the earlier periods of our own, this limit was
often exceeded.^ But under the British rule, in every instance in which the fact of

excessive assessment was proved by large outstanding balances and increased difficulty of realization, the Government has, when the fact was ascertained, taken measures for reducing the assessment.

" The history of our government in India, has been a continued series of reductions of taxation ; and in all the improved systems of revenue administration, of which an account has been given in the preceding part of this paper, the object has been not merely to keep the Government demand witbin the limits of a fair rent, but to leave a large portion of the rent to the proprietors.   In the settlement of the North-West Provinces, the demand was limited to two-thirds of the amount which it appeared, from the best attainable«information, that the land could afford to pay as rent.   The principle which has been, laid down for the next settlement, and acted on whenever resettlement has commenced, is still more liberal: the Government demand is fixed at one-half, instead of two-thirds, of the average net produce; that is, of a fair rent.   The same general standard has been adopted for guidance in the new assess&ent of the Madras territory.   In Bombay no fixed proportion has been kept in view; but the object has been, that land should possess a saleable value.   That this object has been attained throughout the surveyed districts of Bombay, there is full evidence; and as the Ityots have been secured from increase of revenue for the space of 30 years, the value of land may be expected, from the progress of improvement, to be constantly on the increase.

" It has been shown above, that by far the largest item in the public revenue of India is obtained virtually without taxation, because obtained by the mere interception of a payment, which, if not made to the State for public uses, would generally be made to individuals for their private use."

The preceding extract does not make any specific mentiofi of Bengal, or of the Punjab, but it is meant to include these Governments in the general scope of the conclusions it so tersely and justly expresses.   It will be well, however, to complete our view of the whole of the Indian Eevetiue, Tiy briefly observing that in Bengal,— where Lord Cornwallis's Permanent Settlement of 1793, subsequently resurveyed, chiefly prevails—the Land-Tax does not average more than half of a fair net Eental; and that it is stated" upon the most reliable oflicial authority respecting the Punjab—where the Village sy^m of settlement mostly prevails—that from searching and accurate inquiry in the Settlement Department, showing the eract yield and value per acre of every kind of Crop, it has been ascertained that the Government demand does not there exceed one-fifth of the gross value of the produce in rich tracts, and one-sixth, or one-eighth, or even less, in poor tracts of country.

In fact, intentional oppression on the Indian Landholder or cultivator, on the Zumeendar or Eyot, may be put aside as byegone, and as purely a tradition of the past.   The British system of administration has treated the improving* landholders of India, both great and small, with careful consideration; and has exempted them Irom increased assessments on account of improvements, to an extent not known to legislation on Land-Tax in Europe, if indeed we except the permissive powers of Eedemption given in England by Mr. Pitt's Act of 1798.

It may, perhaps, be recollected that in the paper on British Land-Tax Statistics, read to the Statistical Society in May 1857, (see Vol. XX of *Journal,)*, I explained at some length the various logomachies the Land-Tax had given rise to in England from the time of Charles the First, and even before, down to the present period. It is not to be expected that Indian Land-Tax—obviously more complicated—should have been free from the same kind of result. We need not be surprised at the formidable array of volumes of controversial literature it has produced.

If the word Tax, in the ordinary sense of the term, was open to misconstruction as applied to national land revenue in Great Britain—where this impost was a given portion of net reserved rent belonging to the state, and inherited from feudal times—how much more was it so, where applied, as in India, to the integral Kent itself. If England chafed at the burden of a Land-Tax when it was,, at the maximum, One-Fifth of the Net Kent, how could India bear a Tax on the Land, equal to the whole Net Kent, or to more than the whole Net Kent ? The answer is, that reduced to its true definition, Land-Tax does not exist in India. The Kent of the Land is paid to the British Government in India as the sovereign landlord, and by the same right of the strong arm and of the bold wtU as is recognized in the Hindoo laws of Menu, or in those Chapters of the Koran which are the foundation of the Mahometan laws. Even if tlus were disputed, it cannot be denied that the British Government has, *de facto,* 'proprietary rights; but not possessory rights, except for resumed, escheated, or waste, lands. It enjoys the Kent-Koll of the country, but not the power of dispossession of the tenant. And tenants, hereditary but not necessarily resident, form the great mass of the people, whether their tenure be that of members of village communities l cultivators by themselves or deputies; or in any other way. It is only the minority of the people who are Free--holders by inheritance, custom, gift, or purchase.

Dismal relations are sometimes heard of the cruelty of the British Government in India, resuming lands from the ryot when be is unable to pay his Kent or Land Tax. But let us ask if Kesumption has not been the practice from time immemorial in India, and if it be not the condition prevalent in almost every European country in which, by the absence of laws or customs of primogeniture, or by the existence of a fancy for cultivating little patches of ground, the Land is cut up into small freeholds ? This Society -will remember, that in the paper from Lord Lovelace read to them some years ago, this was distinctly pointed out as being the case in France, where frequent resumptions and sales of plots of ground take place to discharge arrears of Land Tax; and even in England timber has, before now, been felled to provide for the arrears of that tax, insignificant, w-e may add, as is its amount, viz.; under One-Hundredth part of the Rental from Real Property.

Having entered into these explanations, we are now in a position to return to the two examples with which we commenced the present paper, of the calculations of incidence of Taxation in India, as set forth in Pari. Paper, 86/'58. Having described the reasons for which it would seem that the Item of Land-Tax must be wholly expunged, if we desire a view of the pressure of Taxation, as distinguished from the Revenue raised per head, we shall find on doing so, that the pressure of Taxation upon each inhabitant, as estimated for 1854-5, was 7id., in the North West Provinces, instead of 3«. 3|J., which are the figures of the Parliamentary Return; and Is. 4(Z. in Bombay Presidency, instead of 3s. in the same return. The further addition which olight to be made for Salt Tax will presently be alluded to.

The corrections thus far have been arrived at by deduction from the figures for the North West Provinces, of the Land Tax for the Financial Tear 1854-5 (given in Pari. Paper 16/'57). In those for Bombay, the Part Paper 86/'58, on which the estimate is based, besides being obviously wrong in Col. 6 of the Table, disagrees in its figures of Col. 4, with those in Pari. Paper 16/ '57, above referred to; and in order to make the amended estimate for Bombay, it has been deemed preferable to take the Sayer, Miscellaneous, Stamps, and Customs Revenues from the latter paper.

But in both instances Salt Duties have been omitted. There is, however, no item of Taxation which so really falls on every individual in India as this one. For salt, ^hen, we must add 3y per head to the *Taxation of the North-West Provinces, which may thzts be estimated at a total of* ll|d. *per head in* 1854-5; and in *Bombay* 5^d. *per head for the same Item, must be added, making the total taxation thers equal to* 1«. 9Jd. *per head.*

Our tot^ estimate of the Pressure of Taxation in 1854-5, is therefore diuerent from the Return made to Parliament in Februasy, 1858, by 2s. 4j<f. per head, or nearly 72 per cent, less than that Return, for the North West Provinces; and by 2s. per head, or nearly 52 per cent, less, for Bombay Presidency.

The comparison between the pressure of Taxation in India, and in the United Kingdom, may with advantage be made in a more general manner. It is in many respects useful to have a clear, approximate view of it. Before commencing such an estimate, it will be desirable to see what is the proportionate density of the population in the two countries.

The following TABLE C affords a convenient and condensed Summary of the Area and Population of British India, and of the Native States immediately connected with the several Presidencies, according to the latest approximate or officially obtained censuses, published by the East India Company.

TABLE C.

SUMMARY *of the* AREA *and*   *of* INDIA. OjBsfrwfetZ *from the*
  "Return of the Area and 'Population of each division of eo/ch Presidenep
  of India, from the latest inquiries; comprising, also, the Area and
  estimated Population of Native States.   Ordered Ip the House of Commons
  to he printed H&th July, 1857."

1	3	8	4	5
States.	Gorersment.	ConotrjpjS.	Total ARKA, in of Square	Total POPULATION, in Millions.
British /	Governor-General of I India in Council....)	I Punjab, Oude, Berar, I Pegu, Tenasserftn,) I Eastern Straits Set \ tlements........................		
	Lieut.-Govemor of) Bengal ....)	(■Upper and Lower Pro- (J vinces, Assam, Ca-1 I char, So.-West Fron- (1 tier, Arracan		
	Lieut.-Governor of1 No.-Westem Pro-> vinces........................J	‚Delhi, Meerut, Agra, Benares, &c., Non- Regulation Provinces, Saugor, Nerbudda, &c..................................		
	Governor of JIadras	‚Madras .Districts, Gan-1 jam, Vizagapatam, Coorg .... J		
	Governor of Bombay	(Bombay District, Sat- 1 tara, Sinde...................		
	с.	*Total,* BRITISH STATES*		
Native J	(Bengal	‚The Deccan, Nepaul, I Bajpoot States, &c......)		
	Madras	Mysore, Travancore, &c.		
	Bombay	I Guzerat and Kattywar,) 1 Petty States, &c.......*I*		
		Total, NATIVB STATES		
		Tbfai, BRITISH AND! NATIVE STATES ..../		

* A correspondent of one of the London papers, " The Daily News," March and April, 1858, in writing on the Organization of our Indian armies, has given some statistics based upon the late redistribution of Indian provinces by Lord Canning, and upon the East India House Tables, of which the above TABLE C is an abstract. They do not differ from the latter materially, and the object in now

The territorial limits of the Political administrations do not quite correspond with those of the Eevenue Collectorates, parts of some of the Presidencies being under the financial rule, or at any rate included in the Eevenue Accounts, of the Governments of other Presidencies. This is of sufficient moment to require the construction of a detailed analysis according to Collectorates, which may also be useful in further statistical enquiries. The results are for convenience transferred to the Appendix (see TABLES N to E, and SUMMABT S, post).

The average population of the British Indian States, as deduced from the figures of which the preceding TABLE C is a summary, may

quoting them is the interesting comparison with the size and populousnesa of several of the great countries of Europe. The writer uses the initials J. B., and we may, with but little risk of error, guess that they belong to a distinguished general officer who is a member of this Society, and has written a great deal on Indian subjects. The following are the hgnres, corrected by those given in the work, India and Europe compared," by Lieut.-General John Briggs. London, 1857, 12 mo.:—

Comparative AREA AND POPULATION *of the Principal Kingdoms of Europe and Her Majesty's Dominions in* INDIA.

Eoaorz.	Area, Sq. Mis.	Population.
Austrian Empire.. 256,784		35,750,621
Kingdom of Bavaria 29,327		4,559,452
	286,111	40,300,075
Empire of France	201,961	35,783,170'
Kingdom of Spain	144,698	14,216,219
Italian States	58,185	10,832,881
	202,883	S_____ iS>o49iioo
Kingdom of Prussia	107,686'	16,331,187.
„ of Holland	13,571	3,397,851
•„ of Saxony	5,759	1,511,272
	127,016	y.2410,3 IO
Naples and Sicily....	42,132	7,975.850
„ Wurtemberg.............	7,503	o ',733,263
•p,	867,606	132,081,768
, INDIA.	222,609	41.961.513
Bengal Presidency ,		24,652,663
Punjaub	112,671	11,790,042
Bombay and Scinde	131,564	36.44i.705
	244,ii5	13.337,033
	74,686	22,437,247
North-West Provinces	132,090	3,460,696
Madras Presidency.......		4,650,000
Mysore............................	30,886	
Nagpore	76,432	8,116,696
	107,3'8	887,151
European settlements	62,993	
	943.9''	I33.«?6,J4S

bo nearly estimated as follows, ranging the "countries in their order of populousness:—

Countries under the Administration of—	Density of Population Per Square Mile.	Proportion Ver Cent, of Tutut Population.
Lieut.-Governor of North-West Provinces	■.318-	*26'*
Lieut.-Govemor of Bengal...	184-	*3 "*
Governor of Madras .... :.....................................	1?0-	**V**
Gov.-General of India in Council (Punjab, *&c.)*	95-	18-
	89-	8-
Average of British India.................-¦	157-	' 100*

The average population of the Indian Empire is 157 per Square Mile, as against 332 per Square Mile for England in 1851. It is, therefore, in the *nggregnte,* not one half as dense. If we are to define it'by the nearest English standard, it may be said to be intermediate between the population of the counties of Northumberland and ^Rutland (154 per Sq. Mile), and of the counties of Salop and Huntingdon (178 per Sq, Mile). But it is denser by 70 per cent, than the population of Scotland (92 per Sq. Mile), and by 16 per cent, than that of Wales (135 per Sq. Mile).   *

Then again, looking at the separate Presidencies in the order of density, we find thet the North West Provinces are thickly peopled, 318 per Sq. Mile, against 332 for the. whcle of England. Or, defining by the nearest parallelism with English Counties, the ratio is intermediate between Derbyshire (288 per Sq. Mile) and Nottinghamshire (329 pe" Sq. Mile).

The population of the Bengal Presidency (184 per Sq. Mile) may be compared, in territorial closeness, with that of the East Riding of York (182 per Sq. Mile), and of Dorset (186 per Sq. Mile).

The population of Madras Presidency (170 per Sq. Mile) ranges between that of Northumberland and Rutland (154 per Sq. MJe), and of Shropshire and Huntingdonshire (178 per Sq, Mile).

The density of population in the Countries under the Governor-General, 95 per Sq. Mile, is to be classed intermediately between that of Westmoreland (77 to the Sq. Mile), and that of the North Riding of Yorkshire (102 to the Sq. Mile),

The most thinly peopled of the Presidencies, Bombay, 89 per Sq. Mile, may also be classed between the English County of Westmoreland and the North Riding of York, just referred to.

For the reasons already mentioned as to the differences between the territorial limits of the Political administrations and of the

Land Revenue Collectxirates, the analysis of the incidence of Taxation per head of the population, may be preferably restricted to a general calculation for the whole of India. As, however, it is useful to show in what parts of India the Items are raised, the following TABLE D "is also arranged for each Presidency;—

TABLE D.

INDIRECT and **DIRECT** TAXATION *of* INDIA *in the Year* 1856-66.

1	3	3	4	6	6	7
	•Presidency or Government.					Whole of India.
Items of Revenue.	Bengal.	No.*-WBtn. Provinces.	Madras.	Bombay.	Punjab.	
(i.) *Indirect Taxation.*	Mlns. £	Mlns. £	Mlns. £	Mlns. £	Mlns. £	Ulns. je
Salt	1-082	-549	•541	•275	•204	x'6si
Customs.	1-541	-078	•140	•348		
Excise	-045		....			•04s
Stamps	-224	-169	•071	•069	•020	'553
	2-892	-796	•752	•692	•224	5'356
Proportion per Cent, of^ Indian Total Indirect Taxation........................J	54'	"S'	'4'	'3'	4'	100*
(ii.) *Mixed, Direct, and Indirect Taxation.*	« 0			* ft		
Sayer and Abkarry (Sondry Taxes, Spirit Licenses, &c.)......................I	-499	-303	•247	•116	•079	J'244
Moturpba (Income Taxi on Artisans, Shop-J keepers, Tool^&c.) J			•109	ft..		■109
	-499	•303	•356	•116	•079	1'353
'Proportion per Cent.	37'	23'	26*	8-	6-	100*
TOTAL *of* (i.) and (ii.)t Indirect and Direct.... I	3-391	1-099	1-108	•808	•303	6-709
Proportions per Cent, ofl (t.) and (ii.) for India'	5'-.	i6*	>7-	12*	4'	100*

It will be observed that thia TABLE D does not include all Items of Indian Revenue. A complete Return of every Item for the Tear 1855-56, being the last for which any definitive results are yet published, has been given in the first TABLE A of the present paper. Here it will sufiice to briefly allude to the reasons for the several

a

omissions, which are requisite in arriving at a just view of Taxation, as distinguished from gross Eevenue Statistics.

The Land Eevenue has already been referred to as really rent, and *not* a Tax. The next Item left out is Post Office Eevenue. This is no Tax, for the rates of Postage are so moderate that they cannot be termed even a remuneration for the services performed by the Government administration of Letter-carriage. The Mint dues, which are trifling in amount, ate also omitted; and similarly with the Miscellaneous Eevenue, not included with what is termed the Sayer Eevenue (which latter is brought into our calculation). The Eevenue technically termed Miscellaneous cannot be taken as a tax upon the body of the people, for the greater part of it is derived from Subsidies of Native Princes, Marine and Pilotage Eeceipts, Judicial Eeceipts, Interest on Debts due, and some small Toll and Ferry Collections. The other Item omitted is Opium Duty. I have left this large Item to be explained last, as I am not aware of any grounds oq which it can be classed among the Taxes of India. It is wholly home by the foreign consumer, and the cultivation of Opium of course helps the payment of all Taxes, by the large employment it gives to native labour and capital.

Eesuming our calculation to be based on TABLES A and B, it win be observed that there is a total Taxation of 6,709,0001., to be distributed amongst 132 Millions of People. Part of this Taxation, the *JUoturpha,* or Income-Tax on Artisans, Shopkeepers, and Stock-in-Trade, has, it is upderstood, subsequently to 1856, been discontinued. We may, therefore, without chance of grave error, take in round numbers 6,600,0001., as the real Taxation home by 132 Millions of Indians subject to the British Eule.

The Average TAXATION *per Head for* INDIA *is therefore* ONE SHILLING.

And for comparison with the United Kingdom, take the Eevenue for the Year ehded 31st March, 1858 (a convenient ^riod as it is the latest, and free from the War Ninepence of additional Income Tax), and we find a total of about 68 Millions. From this amo.iut, and upon the same principles as have been referred to in respect of Indian Fiscal Eevenue, deduct 3 Millions on account of Land Tax and Post-Office Eevenues (say 1 Million for the former and 2 Millions for the latter), and we have 65 Millions left as the Gross Public Taxation, to meet an equivalent amount of the charge of the Consolidated Fund. But w'e may augment this by at least 10 Millions for Local Taxation, including Poor Bates, so that, altogether, there are, at the most moderate calculation, 75 Millions Sterling of positive Taxation to be spread over a population of under 30 Millions of Souls; and of this Taxation, about 64 per cent., or in round terms, a little under two-thirds, are raised by Indirect Taxation; and the remaining 36 per cent., or something over One-third, by Direct Taxation.

The conclusion is, that for GREAT BBITAIN and IBELANI), we have, in sufficiently near approximate figures, an average TAXATION *per head* of at least FIFTY SHILLINGS, against One Shilling per head for India.

There exists, consequently, a Ratio of 50 to 1, if the incidence of taxation proportionately to population be contrasted in the United Kingdom, and in India.

Something like an approach to correctness of judgment upon this point is certainly to be desired. Various public and parliamentary statements, based on such statistical forms as those considered in some detail on this occasion, would indicate an apparent Ratio of only about 9 or 10 to 1.

These differences are not light subjects of inquiry, in which it makes little difference how the balance weighs. It is not "all the same" to One Hundred and Eighty Millions of people, whose condition is affected by the opinions and acts of Thirty Millions of other people.

• The analysis in the following TABLE E will show approximately the distribution of the Taxation of Ono Shilling per head, and the variations in the several parts of India.

Reviewing some of the data in the following TABLE E, it may now be observed, that, taking the Taxation for the whole of British India at Is. per head as the general average rate, the rate per head for Madras is the same; the rate for Bengal and Bombay exceeds it by one-third, being Is. 4d. per head; the rate for the Punjab is one-fourth below it, being *9d.* per head; and, lastly, that the rate for the Nortli-West Provinces is lowest of all, being 7d. per head, or 60 Per Cent, below the general average.

Eevenue from all sources—whether of Tacation or not—being similarly c^pared with the population, it will be seen that the general average for British India being 4s. 8d. per head, the rate fqr Madras is again in close conformity with it, viz.: 4s. *Id.*; that for Bombay the rate is as much as 77 per cent, in excess, being 8s. 3d. per head; for Bengal only about 7 per cent, in excess, viz., 5s. per head; and that in the North-West Provinces and Punjab the rates, viz., 3s. 5d. and 3s. 3d., are about one-third below the general average.

It is conducive to further information, if the proportions between the amount of Eevenue from all sources, and that raised from the particular items only which press upon the people as Taxation,, be ascertained. And upon the evidence of the preceding table, assuming also that the conclusions on which it is based are here admitted, it may be estimated that in the whole of British India *not much, beyond One-Fiftji of the Revenue is raised by Taxation,* or 'say, more nearly 21 Per Cent. In. Bengal 27 per cent, of the revenue is thus raised, being upwards of one-fourth in excess of the general average. In the Punjab 23 per Cent., or about one-tenth in excess. In the

TABLE E,

TAXATION *and* TOTAL REVENUE.—PER CENTAGES *for eaoh* PRESIDENCY; *ani* AVERAQE INCIDENCE PER HEAD *upon the T<adl Populaiiona in the TTear* 1866-56.

	"2	3	4	5	a	7
Description of the Several Calculations.	Bengal.	No.'-Wstn. Provinces.	Madras.	Bombay.	Punjab.	Whole OI Britisb Indi^
	Mlns.	Mlns.	V Mlns.	Mlns.	Mlns.	Mina.
1. Population of the Collectorates in-v eluded in the Revenue Accounts I (see TABLES of Appendix and SUM-j MARIES)	52'	37-	23-	12-	8-	132'
2. *Per. Centage of ditto to Total Indian l Population*	39'	28-	i8-	9'	6-	l00*
3. Taxation, as per TABLE D, *ante,* in\ Millions Sterling, and made up of1 Salt Tax, Customs, Excise, Stamps, | Sayer, Abkarry, and Moturpha ....)	£ 3-391	£ 1099	£ 1-108	£ •808	£ . •303	6";og
4. *Per-Centage of ditto to Total Indian l Taxation*		i6*		12*	4'	l00*
5. Taxation per Head, in Shillings andl Pence, disregarding Fractions.........)	e d. ' 4	de 1'	s, d. t —	9e de ', 4	«. de — 9	8e de 1 —

Supplementary Notes. *Showing the proportion raisldip each Presidency, of the total Revenue from other branches not included in the defnition of Taxa,tion.*

	Per Cent.	Per Cent.	Per Cent.	Per^nt.	Per Cent.	Per Cent.
6. Land Revenue (for amounts, see\ TABLE A)...........	27-	29-	21-	17-	6-	10,0'
7. Opium ditto ditto	80-			20-		l00*
8. Post Office ditto ditto	19-	i*-	25-	9-	io-	l00*
9. Mint Duties ditto	611		10-	29-		l00*
10. Miscellaneous ditto	46-	i-	34-	14-	i-	l00*
	Mlns. £	M-lns. £	Mlns.- £	Mlns.	Mlns.	£
11. Total Revenue from all sources ofl income and taxation l	13019	6-260	5-287	4-953	1-298	30'817
12. Ditto, ditto, per Cent, for each) presidency.....................................)	4i-	20'	i8-	i6'	4-	J00*
	9. d.	S. de	J. de	s. d.	a. de	a, de
13. Ditto, ditto, PER BEAD, in Shillings) and Fence, disregarding Fractions..)	5 --	3, 5	4 1	8 3	3 3	4 8

. North-West Provinces the ratio falls to 17 per cent., or about one-fifth below it. And in Bombay, where, as before observed, the aggregate revenue per head is the highest, the proportion raised from taxation is the lowest, viz., 16 per cent., being one-fourth below the general average.

The figures in TABLE E might also serve to illustrate other matters ; but on the present: occasion it is not desirable to enter on inductions requiring reference to those various methods of land settlement that are prevalent in the several presidencies, and the effects of which are involved in some of the reasons for the differences above pointed out. We have, therefore, restricted the statement to statistical results, and may now conveniently pass to the next branch of inquiry.*

II.—*Productive, financial and industrial condition of the country and people of India. Hegree in which experience and facts have already shown it to he susceptible of improvement through the promotion of agriculture and public works, better means of irrigation and transit by canals and railways, and an amended system of Land Settlement.*

Unquestionable as are the resources of India for the production, on the grandest scale, of articles necessary' and useful in the fdbd and clothing of mankind—important as their development undeniably is to the wealth and position of this country—it is but recently that public attention has been much directed to the promotion of an improvement in this respect. And, indeed, it is scarcely to be wondered at that it-wasp postponed in periods of transition, like those during which the extension and consolidation of the British empire in India absorbed its surplus revenue in the process of military annexation, occupation, and defence.   *i*

The time has, however, arrived when there is a very general hope that a real impetus may be given to the concentration of the energies of its vast, a^d, generally speaking, docile, population, on an effectual pursuit of the arts of peace. Amongst the results to be looked for, are, a more thorough utilization than hitherto of means and opportunities connected with cultivation, trade, and industry—a better supply of raw produce to our markets at home—an increased importation of British manufactured goods—an avoidance of the extreme evils from the periodical scarcities of food which are apt to decimate portions of the Indian population—and, finally, an improvement of its moral and spiritual condition through a gradual elevation of its physical and material status.

A preservation of the dead level of the existing state of things is most earnestly to be deprecated. Exhaustion of resources in an unproductive manner has been for ages upon ages the bane of India. It is within the power of British administration to show that this can be reversed: and that a country which, with all the material of wealth, is eminently poor, can be made rich in every sense of the word.

The problem is not simply the raising of a larger revenue. This was solved by the old Mahomedan sovereigns, who found ways of levying a larger amount than the present Revenues of India, upon a smaller territory; from probably a less population; and certainly with commercial and fiscal circumstances inferior to those which now exist. But the real problem is, to do away with the exhaustive social condition of the people of Indian. To accomplish this, the illusion of the balance of trade theory must be entirely swept away. It is not a question of the precious metals. For thousands of years India has absorbed silver and gold to an extent which has. alarmed that section of ancient and modem bullionists, to whom these two metals are exclusive incarnations, as it were, of wealth.

In a country like India, where—under the old regime—oppression, wasted energy, unproductive expenditure, deadening influence of caste, early marriages and polygamy, have prevailed, a golden stream, even though it rivalled that of Pactolus, might have flowed in vain. We must never lose sight of the fact, that " king's barbaric," notwithstanding the " pearl and gold," were the ruin of India. The high-caste Babfi, lolling in his carriage in the streets of Calcutta, is said often to sigh for the days of the Delhi Moguls—the glitter and show of their courts and camps, and the elegant and costly monuments they reared. 'But is the reverse of the picture considered? a reverse, with few exceptions, painted in the darkest colours even by historians whose bias was in favour of a system which the facta they recite utterly condemn. Hoads were, it is true, constructed, but in wholly insufiScient quantity; great arteries of communication were opened up, but the veins and feeders of them were neglected. The direction of the roads also was dictated rather by^ponveuieiice of strategic purpose, or the personal comfort of the sovereign, than by the view of development of the resources and well-being of the people. Stately buildings were erected for palaces, halting places and tombs; works intended to exalt the name, and perpetuate the personal vanity of sovereigns who generally left unfinished what had been begun before them, in order to embark in fresh and more wasteful undertakings, doomed in turn to be neglected by their successors.

It is not to be supposed that, in the long period of seven centuries of Mahomedan government, rulers exceptionally superior should not have appeared ; but the instances are few, and the foundations of a wise and settled financial policy were never laid. The skill and wisdom of an administrator like Akbar, supported as it was by the great Finance ministers who settled his revenue scheme, failed to subvert the system of oriental statecraft which had its roots in fear, and not in mutual support, and possessed qualities which might make it flourish for a time, but left the elements of stability and of progressive prosperity wanting.

Some canals, and other productive public works, were certainly constructed; but the revenue was chiefly spent in devastating and impoverishing war, and in the unbridled indulgence of the sovereign, his favourites, an4 his Tax gatherers. ı In expenditure, wasteful as it usually was, a good effect was nevertheless apparent on the surface. It employed labour. It incasased the circulation of money. The public treasury always derived a passing benefit from such circumstances. The period,was one of "full currency," in which the channels of taxation were easier filled. But the effect was transient; the reaction—of diminished employment of labour—of want of adequate return from the objects on which the capital was expended—of restricted circulation of money—soon set in; and then tyranny and exaction were always ready ttf fill the void and force the supplies.*

Mr. Arthur Mills, M.P., in his recent work "India in 1858," f has given some approximate figures of the items of Expenditure of the Government of India, which it will be well to refer to here, as neither the limits nor the objects of this paper will admit of more than a passing note of the general statistics of expenditure. The figures are given by Mr. Mills, in the following round numbers, and I,,, have here annexed the per centages borne by each item to the total. The estimate is made on an average of four years preceding the Mutiny of 1857-8.

		PCT Cent, of Total Expenses.
Charges incident to the collection of the Revenue	6,000,000	. ... 20*
Military and Naval Charges...	11,000,000	.
Civil, Judicial, and Police.................. „................................	5,000,000	. ∨
Public Works...	1,'500,000	., 5.
Interest on l^nd Debt in India	2,000,000	. T
Charges defrayed in England (including interest' on home bond debt, dividends to proprietors of i East India Stock, amounting in the last estimated return to 627,8932.); Payments on account ı of Her Majesty's Troops, and establishment charges at the East India House and Board of Control	3,500,000	. ... ir
Allowances and assignments to Native Princes,! under treaties and other engagements....................f	1,000,000	. ... .3*
Total, about...........'..................	30,000,000	.... ICO*

* " Faites passer beaucoup d'argent par les mains du people, il en reflue n4ccs. sairement, dans le tr^sor, une quantity proportionnee que personne ne regrette. Le people a-t-il pen d'argent, il en rendra pen, et il faudra le lui arracher."—*Porbonnais.*

t London, Murray, 1858. See p. 133 of second edition.

The only item which need he now referred to, is that of Public Works, which, it will be observed, is only 5 per cent, of the total expenditure, although as Landlords, or at least as chief receivers of Eent, the government are mainly interested in that branch of expenditure.

In the paper read to this Society in January last, by our Vice-President, Colonel Sykes, M.P., on " Public Works in India," the nature and extent of the improvements in late years of the British administration of public works in India, is elaborately described. Besides the many valuable Indian Statistics for which this Society and its Transactions have been indebted, on that and on many previous occasions, to the experience and industry of Colonel Sykes, reference may also be made on the general subject of the recent policy of the East India Company, in respect of public works (such as the Ganges Canal, the Telegraph, Eailways, &c.), to Lord Dalhousie's well-known Memorandum, and to the documents which have emanated from the East India House, and do great credit to its Statistical department.

The expenditure on public works in India may have been shown to be judicious; its results in the profitable return of interest, directly or indirectly, on the capital expended, have proved satisfactory, and in some- instances, surprisingly so. It may be evidenced that more has been efiected for the good of the people of India than the Mahomedan system of expenditure could accomplish; but we must not conceal from ourselves the fact, that in number, extent, and outlay, the experimental public works, already undertaken and finished, have fallen short of what is desirable, and in some respects necessary, when we consider the extent of area and population whose material progress is concerned.

The great machinery of credit, capital, and industry, according to the methods and views adopted in the United Kingdom and in the United States, must be brought to bear with far greater-rapidity, and in much more extensive and connected a manner than hitherto, if the British possession of India is to be made reciprocally advantageous to its people and ourselves.

A member of this Society, Dr. Hyde Clarke, has recently published a work on " Indian Colonization, Defence, and Eailways," * the 13th chapter of which treats on the operations of English Capital in India, particularly with reference to railways. The whole work, and especially the chapter referred to, is well worthy of attentive consideration. The author shows (1) that there is no question connected with labour and capital, and involved in the construction of railways and public works (either in this country or in America),

* London, Weale, 1857. See pp. 184 to 224. Consult also Lieut.-Colonel Kennedy's pamphlet on analogous subjects. London, Wilson, 1858.

wliich has not been satisfactorily answered by the teaching of results as beneficial as they are important; and (2) that similar results are ı equally to be looked for in India. " That no labourer need be im-" ported there; no food, no clothing for the.labourer need be imported; " but what is required is to direct the labour of one hundred and " fifty millions of people, whose time is now chiefly spent in inactivity, " so as to construct the required railway, canal, irrigating and other "public works;" for though, as Dr. •Clarke proceeds to say, he has treated the subject in direct reference' to railways, " it equally applies " to all those public works advocated in preference to railways by "their opponents, and it shows whence the means are forthcoming "for endowing India with every requisite means of advancement, " namely, by the rightftil application of her own energies and re-" sources, without putting a veto on any branch of enterprise."   •

Positive experience already gained respecting Canals and Irriga-tion, and the improvement of Rivers and Inland Navigation, has been vei'y striking.   In Colonel Sykes's " Notes bn Public Works in India," this Society will recollect that it was observed that the amount of Interest shown by the net revenue from the Delhi and Western Jumna Canals, is 36 per cent, on the invested capital; that the Doab or Eastern Jumna Canal gives a net annual return on the capital laid out, of nearly 24 per cent.; that the return to be expected from the expenditure in progress of 1| Million Sterling on the Ganges Canal, will be 28 per cent.   The locality of these three undertakings is in the North-West Provinaes. •

The dry arithmetical ■statement of the per centage return on invested capital is, however, by no means the measure of all the good accomplished.   The productiveness of the land, and the consequent increase of the Rent or Land Revenue of the Goverurj'eht, has uniformly augmented largely and immediately under the improve-ment of irrigation and transit, as affecting cultivation, water power, grazing, &c.? and lastly, though far from least noticeable, is the fact that the premature death of thousands of persons from famine has been averted, and wealth to the extent of Millions of Pounds Sterling has been preserved, as well as produced, through the self-same means.

Comparatively with area and population, the extension of these works has not been either so great or so continuous as might be desired.   If we exclude those undertakings. that are of a purely military character, and review the items which may be classed under Land and Water channels of communication and Irrigation Works, or in other words, the Revenue-productive Public Works, in recent years of most activity, it appears that an outlay of about One Million and a Half Sterling has been the maximum for one year.   If we take the most immediately productive works, viz.: of Canalization and

Irrigation, it will be seen that not more than, 738,015Z, in the year 1853-54, and 543,333Z. in the year 1854-55, was thus expended.*

The condition of the Eevenue, as preventing a more rapid and extensive outlay, has hitherto been an answer to those who might have been disposed to urge that even these amounts are insignificant, when the British Indian territory of 837,000 Square Miles, and its 132,000,000 of souls are considered.   This answer resolves itself purely into one of alleged financial difficulty.   That this difficulty is only apparent, and might be remedied, is evident, not only from the practical testimony of the productive results of such expenditure in the instances before adverted to, but also from the history and policy of the other branches of the Colonial Empire of this country.   And the history of the East India Company, or of the trading companies of other countries, has shown no exception to the general rule, that expenditure on carefuUy selected objects of enterprise may often appear lavish and profuse, when it is but sowing the field whose harvest is the proof of the wise economy of that expenditure.

In the matter of the provision of Funds for Eailway construction in India, we have an example of the deepest moment in proving that even the condition of some deferment of any large return for money expended, is no efiectual bar to the ways and means of enterprise. During the eight years since the system of Indian Eailways was started, only between two and three hundred miles of line have been opened for traffic.   So far as the cost is concerned, the figures given in TXBLE VII of Colond Sykes's paper are confined to the two sections of Calcutta to Eaneegunge," on the East Indian line, 121 miles, at about *12,000l.* per mile; and of Madras to Arat, on the Madras line, 65 miles, at about 5,050Z. per mile.   The cost of the complete'd portion of the Bombay and Baroda line is not yet known. Eestricting our observation, therefore, to the first two examples that are known, the experimental results of an aggregate outlay of 1,780,0001. only, can yet bo observed.   Of this, the SUm of about 1,452,0001., being the outlay from Calcutta to Eaneegunge, is said to be earning 7 per cent.

The sum paid by Eailway Companies into the Treasury of the East India Company in England and India, is about 14J Millions Sterling, out of a total amount of nearly 23 Millions Sterling authorized to be raised as at the close of the year 1857.

If then, imder the system of guarantee, the resources of credit have led to the utilization of so important an amount of capital in a

---

* These are the figures under the Classifications of *Reeenue and Irrigation,*— (Canals, Tanka, Emhankments, Drainage, &c.),—and of *Repairs* of the like items. Under the classification *Ptthlic,* Navigable Canals also occur, but the amount so included did not reach 8,0001. in the year 1853-54.—See Colonel Sykes's paper already referred to.

direction which, useful as it is, and highly to he applauded, is not so largely and so immediately profitable as some other descriptions of Public Works in India, there is no reason why the latter should not be promoted and increased at the same time and by the same methods.

The examples already quoted from the paper by Colonel Sykes, on " Public Works in India," indicate some of the Results from the Canal and Irrigation Works in the North-West Provinces. Results of an equally encouraging character are also given in the same paper, as having been experienced in the Madras Presidency. The detailed tables of the special and other original works of irrigation performed in that part of India, and showing the effects upon Eevenue and Cultivation from 1836 to* 1849, are confirmatory of the statistics and, views respecting them published by Colonel Arthur Cotton, who has for many years upheld the promotion of a deeper sense than is com-/ monly entertained, of the responsibilities inseparable from the British rule in India, and of the absolute necessity for a more ample develop-^ ment of the material and moral resources of the soil and people with, which Providence has connected it.*

In the first part of the present paper it was endeavoured to be shown what part of the Eevenue of India depends on Taxation pressing upon the people, and what part upon Eent, or upon the net produce of the cultivation of the soil. It will be recollected that grounds were adduced on which to estimate the Taxation at only 21 per cent, of the gross Eevenue; and data Were |pven for rating fiSj per cent, of the gross EevfinueJ as derived from reserved rent, or so termed Land Tax. These are proportions which, compared with those existing in other countries, justify a very hopeful view of the peculiar adaptability of the Eevenue of India to profit promptly and decisively from an increased momentum being ^iven to productive expenditure.

In most countries the temporary or permanent burden of a fresh Loan, whether for productive outlay or not, must be borne by the

---

* Colonel Arthur Cotton's book, " Public Works in India, their importance, with suggestions for their extension and improvement," was first written for private circulation in India. A second edition, considerably augmented, was published in London in 1854. During Colonel Arthur Cotton's stay in England, in 1856, he published a pamphlet entitled " Profits upon British Capital expended on Indian public works, as shown by the results of the Godavery Delta Works of Irrigation and Navigation." The statistics and general conclusions of this pamphlet deserve attention. As regards Railway Expenditure and the policy of Railway construction in India, 1 am certainly on the side of those who differ, to a certain extent, with Colonel Arthur Cotton, but need not assure him of the respect which I entertain for his judgment, experience, and largeness of view, upon all points that tend to advance the resources and condition of those parts of India where his labours have worked so much good.

iraposition of Taxation.   In India, unproductive expenditure only such as defensive or aggressive war, or administrative extravagance, would likewise have to be thus defrayed, and in no country would it be more difiBcult to augment taxation for such purposes.   But how differently circumstanced the conditions are with respect to outlay for industrial purposes in India, as compared with other countries, is obvious from the single circumstance of 55} per cent, of the gross Eevenue, being as stated. Eent of Land, a proportion far larger than in other parts of the world, and an Item of Eevenue which all experience has shown is more easily inq)rovable than any other, by productive expenditure devoted to reclaiming and improving; to " making war" (as the American phrase has it) "upon the wilderness"; , to rendering rivers navigable, and watercourses and wells useful in irrigation; to bringing out the latent capabilities of the'country for 'the growth of cotton, sugar, rice, indigo, silk, fibres, &c.

The old-fashioned and true doctrine, that, in State finance, *"pardmoniaf* was nationally a *" magnwm vectigal,"* was mistakenly exaggerated by the opponents of the funding system in England, such as Er. Price and his followers, into a groundless fear that all borrowing and employment of the machinery of credit was opposed to that doctrine.   They refused to look around and take a large and practical view of the even then accumulated experience of European countries, whose' resources had been increased, in every respect, though judicious expenditure of means raised upon an anticipation of the productive and profitable results which those means themselves in due season created.

And so would it be in India, under European guidance and discreet management.   A Public Works Loan in India, under such a local aid home administration as would afford a guarantee for its employment to the best advantage, would meet with a ready, and (it may be termed) a national, response, from the Indian native capitalists who might, when the right moment arrives, be inVited to subscribe for a given portion of the Loan.   A body of small capitalists might also be encouraged, and every Stockholder amongst them would be a further guarantee for the peace and welfare of the Indian community at large.

In continuation of the Statistics of the subject before us, the annexed TABLE P contains a statement of the Indian Debt in the several Presidencies, and of the Home Debt, according to the latest returns obtainable.   The Statement following it, viz., TABLE G-, gives an analysis of the Indian Debt into its several categories of Loans, Deposits, &c.

TABLE F.

PCULIC DEBTS *of the* PRESIDENCIES *of* INDIA *and* HOME DEBTS *of the* EAST
INDIA COUPANT; *as at Zdth April,* 1856.*

Amounts converted into Sterling Mtmeg at the rate of Is, 10|<Z. *per Comptang's
Rupee.*

	3	3	4
	Amount of Debt.	Bate of Interest.	Annual Amount of Interest.
INDIAN DEBT.			
(i.) *Bengal.*	£	Per Cent.	£
LOANS.	338,178	6	20,291
Ditto .	3,744,141	5	187,207
Ditto .	39,392,841	4	I.575-7I4
Ditto .	530,730	3i	18.575
	44,005,890	Avg. 4'095	1,801,787
LOAN transferred from Fort Marlborough	715	10	71
Treasury Notes	9171133	6, 4, & 33	37.097
Civil and Medical Funds	2,268,300	6, 5, & 4	135.789
Miscellaneous Deposits.........	106,166	3 '	3.18s
	47,298,204	Avg. 4'182	1.977,9^9
(II.) *North-Western Provinces, including the annexed Territory.*			
Miscellaneous Deposits.........	18,750	•4	750
Temporary LOANS.........	219,656	5	10,982
	238,406	Avg. 4'921	II.73J
(HI.) *Madras.*			III
LOANS.	14,437,	8	*ii'SS*
DITTO .	7,547	6	453
Civil, Military, and Medical Funds	839,330	6 & 5	46.981
Miscellaneous Deposits	77,755	6,5,4,33&3	2,779
Treasury Notes	49,172	4 & 33	1,960
Fund for Redemption of Bonds issued tol Creditors of the late Rajah of Tanjore .... /	395,423	4	. • r'5.8i7
	1,383,664	Avg. 5	69.145
(?v.) *Bombay.*			
Civil Annuity and other Funds........	568,019	6	34.08l
Civil Provident and Military Funds	881,287	5	44.064
Miscellaneous Deposits.........	112,383	3 & 4	3.573
Treasury Notes	1,406		53
	1,563,095	Avg. 5'231	81,771
{y.) *Punjab.*			....
TOTAL. INDIAN DEBT	50,483,369	Avg. 43	2,140.577

* The materials upon which this estimate is based are from the Official accounts
(Pari, papers, 135 and 110, Session 2 of 1857).   From the Lords' Returns to Lord
Monteagle's motion of 18th Feb., 1858, it appears that no accounts for the year
1856-7 had been received at the East India House.   As regards the Home Bond
Debt, the Return (44) to the Earl of Ellenborough's motion of 15th March, 1858,
confirms the figures as above.   *

TABLE F.—*Continued.*

1		3	4
	Amount of Debt.	Koto of Interest.	Annual Amount of Interest.
HOME DEBT.		Per Cent.	£
East India Stock, 6 Millions Sterling of 101 per Cent. Stock, redeemable at 12/ Millions..............	12,000,000^	(5| on • redemption price.)	$1 6^0,000$
Home Bond Debt, charged upon the revenues of India by 3 & 4 Will. IV, c. 85 (20,9171. of the Principal not bearing Interest)..........o	3,915,317	4	155.776
TOTAL HOME DEBT	15,915,317	Avg. 4'908	785.756
TOTAL INDIAN AND HOME DEBT	66,398,686	Avg. 4'408	1.926,353

TABLE 6.

ANALYSIS *of the* ITEMS *constituting the* PUBLIC DEBTS *of the* PRESIDENCIES 0/ INDIA; 0S *at SOth April,* 1856, (exclusive of Railway Funds or Guarantees.)

1	2	3	•i	6
	Debt.		Interest.	
Classificutiou of Items.	Amount.	Proportion of Total Debt.	Amount of AiinunI Cborge.	Kate of Interest.
	Mlns. £	Per Cent.	Mlns.	Per Cent.
1. Loans　　　J	44-029	87-11	1-803	4'095
2. Temporary Loans .	9-219.	o'+3	0-011	5-000
3. Treasury Notes	0-968	*vgz*	0-039	4'041
4. Ileulmption Fund of Bond Debt ...	0-395	*0-78*	0-016	4'000
5. Miscellaneous Deposits	0-315	0-63	0-010	3'263
G. Civil, Military, and Medical Provi-1 dent and Annuity Funds...................>	4-557	9'03	U-261	5'725
Total, Indian Debt,,	50-483	100'00	2-140	

Proportions of the Debts of the several Presidencies.	Mlns. £	Per Centn^c of Total.	Mlns. je	Percentage of Total.
I.—Bengal..	47-298	93'69	1-978	92'44
II.—North-West Provinces.	0-238	0'47	0-011	0-51
HI.—Madras.	1-384	2'7+	0-069	3'22
IV.—Bombay	1-563	3'>o	0-082	3'83
V.—Punjab .				
Total, Indian Debt.	50-483	100'00	2-140	100'00

The preceding TABLE F shows, that the total annual charge for the year ended 30th April, 1856; or, in other words, the aggregate amount of annual interest, may be classed in the following three great divisions:—

	£
Interest on the Indian Debt	2,140,577
Dividends to Proprietors of Stock.	630,000
Interest on the Home Bond Debt.	155,776
Total	**2,926,353**

Sir George Comewall Lewis in his speech (Committee of the House of Commons on the East India Loan Bill, 22nd Eebruaiy, 1858), in referring to the state of the total annual charge, according to the last accounts presented to Parliament, at the date to which the above figures apply, gave the amounts as follows:—

	£
Interest on the Indian Debt	2,044,318
Dividends to Proprietors of Stock	632,089
Interest on the Home Bond Debt	152,017
Total	**2.828,424**

But these are the figures of the interest paid in the year ended 30th April, 1856, and seem to have been quoted by mistake, for the figures of the annual charge imposed by the debt, which, as first above given, are 97,929/1. per annum more than those in the ex-Chancellor of the Exchequer's statement.

It has already been repeated that no detailed accounts of the Revenue and Debt, yet published, extend beyond the date of 30th April, 1856. So far, however, as the principal of the Indian Public Debt is concerned, we are enabled, upon the authority of j Larliamentary Return published at the close of the present month (April 1858), to bring down some of Sir G. C. Lewis's figures to a later date, and those will be referred to hereafter.

The Right Hon. Gentleman stated the principal sum of the several branches of debt to be as follows:—

" That stock (of the East India Company) amounts to 6,000,000/., and is guaranteed at 12,000,000/.,—that is to say, 200/. are to be paid for every 100/.,—so that the whole sum may be considered as equivalent to a debt of 12,000,000/. Now, tlie guarantee fund which is to be set off against that debt amounts to about 4,500,000/., and we reckon that it will, in the course of a few years, be as high as 7,000,000/. Well, the India debt—in respect of all the three Presidencies—is 50.483,000/., and the Bond Debt about 6,000,000/.; those various sums, in conjunction, constituting a total charge of 68,000,000/. That is the whole of the present charge upon the revenues of India, and against that is to be set off the guarantee fund. The Committee will therefore see that, comparing the gross debt of India with its annual revenue—which is 29,000,000/.—the amount is not so considerable as might have been suppos^."

It will be observed that Sir G. C. Lewis gives the amount of the Home Bond Debt at about 6,000,000*l*., whilst the corresponding figures in TABLE D are 3,916,317*l*. The latter figures agree with those in the Return to the Order of the House of Lords, dated 15th March, 1858. It will not, therefore, be technically correct to assume the Bond Debt at 6,000,000*l*. It is true it appears in the Return just mentioned, that in addition to the Bond Debt of 3,915,317*l*., there was, on the Slst January, 1858, a Debt of the East India Company, for " Money borrowed on security of East India Bonds," amounting to 1,970,000*l*. And the two sums together, viz., 3,915,317*l*., and 1,970,000*l*., make up 5,885,317*l*., which may fairly be presumed as the items constituting the amount of about 6,000,000*l*. ' alluded to by Sir G. C. Lewis.

The Bonds of the Home Debt are issued at *4 Per Cent.,* and redeemable upon a year's notice, and the limit of the borrowing powers extends to 7,000,000*l*. of such bonds. The debt of 1,970,000*l*., on security of East India Bonds may, for aU that appears on the face of the accounts, be chargeable with a very different rate, of interest, and its repayment not be subject to the year's notice. The estimate of the Receipts and Disbursements of the Home Treasury of the East India Company from 1st May of the present year (1858) to 30th April, 1859, sets forth, " Dividends to proprietors of East " India Stock,", 630,000*l*.;' " Interest on the Home Bond Debt," 150,000*l*.; and finally, " *Interest on Honey boi-roicedf* J 20,000*l*. This last item marks the distinction between the temporary, or banking, accommodation, of Loans oij, security of East India Bonds, and ordinary Bonds positively issued. If a Loan had not been on the point of negotiation with the view of covering the whole of the estiniiicvd. deficiencies of the year 1858-59, this distinction might not be worth insisting on. If, however,' we are to arrive at anything like an approximate view of the real amount of Indian Debt as at the present time, we must keep in recollection that the bans on which . the new Indian Loan of eight Millions has just been contracted, included provision against the liability to repay in October 1858, 1,000,009*l*. borrowed of the Bank of England, and 653,000*l*. of Bonds.

Ou the grounds set forth, it is preferred to retain the figures in TABLE F of 3,915,317*l*. as the amount of the Home Bond Debt:

It has already been observed that some later returns are now available* as to the Public debt of the Presidencies, which has hitherto been the chief means resorted to of covering deficits. This return states, that in addition to the Total Indian Debt at Interest on the Ist May, 1856, viz., 50,483,369*l*. (see TABLE F *ante),* the following Loans have been opened:—

♦ **East India (Public Debt) Return to Mr. Crawford's motion. Ordered to be printed 13th April, 1858. No. 179.**

Pour-nnd-a-Half per Cent. Loan, opened 30th August, 1856, closed) ocoisy
16th January, 1857. Subscriptions in cash ....**f**
Five per Cent. Loan, opened 16th January, 1857. Sub-) –qo
scriptions in cash to 20th February, 1858. ....J
Subscriptions in paper of the Three-and-a-half, Four,!
and Four-and-a-half per Cent. Loans, to. 20th Fe-> 1,877,959
bruary, 1858 ....J
                                                            ------------- 5,666,747

Total raised between 30th April, 1856, and 20th February, 1858 6,034,884

This brings up the Public Indian Debt of the Presidencies to the aggregate amount of 56,518,253*l*., and the annual charge of interest thereon to 2,440,480*l*. ı   *

. And the data are now available for arriving at a more precise statistical view of the whole debt at* the charge of the. territorial revenues of India, than can be referred to in any published form.

Avoiding fractions of a thousand pounds, we arrive at the following summary

Summaty of Public Debts {April, 1858,) *including all DAts autkoriged to ba raised.*

Principal of Debt.		Anaual Charge f<tf Interest.
£		£
56.518,000	East Indian Public Debt of the Presidencies........................	2,440,000
3,916,000	Home Bond Debt..	156,000
8,000,000	| East Indian Loan of 1858 (now being raised, 5 Millions| ' immediately, «. e., between 5th April and 15th Sept.,) (1858, and 3 Millions \jlien convenient)........................j	320,000
68,434,000	Total charge on Indian Revenues exclusively........................	2,916,000
7,500,000	[Capital Stock-of the East India Company charged on the 1 Indian Revenues primarily, but guaranteed by the 4 Imperial Exchequer, 6 Millions of Stock, redeemable 1 at 12 Millions, of which it appears 4| Millions are (already accumulated, leaving to provide, ne^..............	630,000
75»934i0OO	ƒT^al Indian and Home Public Debts of the East India) (Company 1	3,546,000

Q

The accumulation of Cebfc, even- including the extraordinary expenses pf the Afghan, Punjab, and Sinde wars, and a large part of the charges of the Indian Mutiny of J857-58, has been by no means so rapid as is frequently taken for granted by persons who profess an aversion from statistical inquiries.

Nothing can be more erroneous than the notion—(which, somehow or other, has widely spread)—that IJie Indian Territorial and Home Debt had been largely increasing in recent years before the mutiny, and that the finances of India have betrayed a chronic, incurable state of deficiency.   •

.C

The increase in the nominal capital of the debt, has, all things considered, been moderate, and it is not the only, nor by any means the most important, point to be inquired into, for in a public debt, or in other words, in a mortgage of Eevenue and Taxes, the amount of annual charge is the true test of the ratio of increase.

It will be desirable to make a comparison between the Capital and annual charge for interest on the Debts of all kinds, at 1st May, 1834, which date is immediately after' the cessation of the Company's trading privileges (under the Act of Parliament 3 & 4 Will. IV, c. 85, taking effect as from 22nd April, 1834), and the capital and annual charge at 1st MaTy, 1858.

1	2‘	S*	4
East Indian Public Debts on 1st May, 1834.	Amfrant.	Kate of Interest.	Annual Charge for Interest.
	£	Per Cent.	
Loans transferred from Fort Marlborough	1,851	10	
Madras Permanent Loan	14,437	8	1.155
Remittable Debt, 30tb June, 1822	7,474,210		
Loan from King of Oude	563,909		
Stipend Fund of the Bhow Begum	607,927		
Madras Notes, under Advertisement, May 11	85,018		
Madras Permanent Loan	10,137		
Total of 6 per Cent. Loans....	8,741,201		514.472
Loan of 31st March, 1823	4,691,920	5	
Loan of 1825-26 ....ft,.......	7,840,080		
Loan of 1829-30 .... •w	L697,68O		
Loan from King of Oude...	1,553,965		
Loan from Individuals........	28,515		
Total of 5 *per* Cent. Loans....	15,812,160		790,608
Loan from Mabaruck Ool Nissa Begum.	1,627	4	
Loan of 1824-25	123,110		
Loan of 1828-29	52,120		
Loan of 1832-33	5,104,850		
Loan from King of Oude	315,769		
Ditto Xlharity Fund	28,706		
Total of 4 per Cent. Ixions ...	5,626,182		225.047
ɪ *Grand Total of the above* Registered Debts....	30,195,831	Avg. Sᴛ's .	b54>.4<'7
Temporary Loans			
Treasury Notes	599,830	Estimatd.	
Deposits, including the Carnatic and otherl Funds —*f*	4,667,822	Avg. 4i J	23«.57ot
Total Indian Debt, at Interest	35,463,483	A<ig. 5	1.778,037

* Cols, 2 and 3 are from East Indis House Return of 9th April, 1858.

t This last Item can only be Cbtimated by the charge of the year. 11 cannot, however, be materially inexact.   *

The data have now been collected for a sufficiently near approximate estimate of the comparative Debt and net annual Interest thereon at the two periods.   These may be conveniently arranged as follows;—

Summary ofPMie Debts at lat *May,* 1834, *and* lat *May,* 1858.

■Capital of Debt.			Annual Interest.	
In 1834.	In 1858.		In 1834.	In 1858.
£	£		£	£
35,463,000	*36,518,000*	/East Indian Public Debt of tliel I Presidencies..................................)	1,778,000	2,440,000
	3,916,000	Home Bond Debt........		156,000
....	8,000,000*	I Ea^ Indian Loans under special l (Acts of Parliament....................)		•ji0.000
35,463,000	68,434»°o°		1,778,000	2,916,000
12,000,000	7,50o,ooo-|-	(Capital Stock of the East India) 1 Company, less the accumu-> 1 lated Guarantee Fund...............J	630,000	t495.000
47.463,000	7S'934->°°°	Totals	2,408,000	3,411,000
....	28,471,000	/Differences, more in 1858 than) 1 in 1834 ..../	....	1,003,000
	60*	Per Cent, more in do. do....		42*

Whilst the increase in the nominal capital of the Debt has thus been about 28J Millions Sterling in 24 years, or ,60 Per Cent, the increase in the annual change for Interest has only been about 1 Million Sterling, or 42 Per Cent.   This difference in the per centages is accounted for chiefly by the improvement of the credit of the British administration in India, as indicated by the calcidatibns respecting the average rate of interest payable on the Loans of the Presidencies, which in 1834, as has just been shown, was about 6 per cent., and in 1858, about 4| per cent.

Adhering to our former proposition that the comparison of the annual charge for interest is more effectual and correct, than any comparison of the nominal principal of a Public Loan; let us now briefly investigate whether the augmentation of 42 Per Cent, in the Interest Charge on the Debt, in the 24 years since the East India Company ceased to possess its trading privileges—*i. e.,* in the period from 1st May, 1834, to 1st May, 1859—has been excessive or not.

◆ Including the charge for the whole of the 8,000,000/. proposed to be raised for the service of the year, 1858-9.

f This item is given at a different amount at the two periods, because in a comparative statement of this kind it is necessary to credit the liability to Proprietors' Capital and Interest by tlie accumulated Capital and Interest on the Redemption of Capital Guarantee Fund.

c *2*

One of the chief statistical standards for estimating this, is obviously,: the Revenue at each of these dates!.

Now,.the gross Indian Eevenue for the year 1833-34- was about 18i Millions; and the estimate of the Gross Indian Revenue for the year 1857-58 may, on the- best, available, authority, be taken at about 29 Millions sterling. The increase in the Revenue has there- fore been 59 per cent.

The ratio of increase of the Revenue has, if is plain, been 17 per cent, more -rapid than the ratio of increase in the charge of the Debt, notwithstanding the largo expenses which have been defrayed, during tlie Twenty-Four Years 1834-1'858, in the annexation, settle- ment, arid survey, of several vast territories and populations; and notwithstanding the charges of arresting offensive wars and muti- nies. And if, further, we take into consideration the fact, that the foundations of useful, prudent, and productive enterprises and works have almost exclusively been laid during this period of time, and some of them brought to a successful completion, we shall not he' justified in agreeing with those' who sweepingly assert that the Finances of British India have long been on the decline.

It is Well known to those who will take the trouble of reflecting on the facts of the Indian Revenue, that the deficits of the last few years wquld not have existed had it not been for the increased expenditure on productive Public Works, which (aa set forth in Colonel Sykes's Paper read to this Society in January last), amounted, exclusive of Military Works, to about One Million and a Half Sterlipg duping each of the four years included in his obser- vations. The Chairman of the EastIndia Company has subsequently quoted some statistics to the House of Coinmous, which extend the figured a little further in date. The following are his remarks, as reported:—

"The statement he (Mr. Mangles) was about to read to the Committee undoubtedly contained some military works which were not a remunerative character; but, on the other hand, nothing was charged for the repairs, or for tlie salaries of the engineering officers by whom the whole had been carried out. The one might, therefore, he set against the other.

		Revenue. £	Public Works. £ '
1852-3	Surplus	424,257	592,516
1853-4	Deficit	2,044,117	952,10.3
1854-5	....	1,707,364	1,818,978
1855-C	,,................	972,791	2,279.539
1856-7	,,	1,981,062	1,839,575
	Total Deficit........	6,281,077	>,474,711

" Thus in the last five years upwards of a. million sterling has been expended in public works more than was required to make the revenue balance.''*

* See debate in Committee on the Resolutions upon tlie Government of India. 30th April, C858.

lu considering Statistics of this kind, the Statistical Society should not neglect to notice that a loan was raised in India in March 1855 ; which, at Is. lOJrf. per Company's Rupee, represented a Sum of 2,577,141*l.* Sterling, expressly in aid of Public Works. It cannot, therefore, be maintained that there was positively no real immediate deficit in the 5 years 1852-3 to 1856-7. Still, the admission cannot in fairness he refused, that a deficit thus arising, is, (paradoxical as it may seem in the crude statement,) capital invested, and probably well invested; for all experience leads to the belief that the best method of lightening the burdens of the people of India, is the timely and. energetic use of the powerful element of public credit applied with special regard to the Wants and resoitrces of the country.   •

Indian financiers (as I hope to show in the next section of this paper), have long been profound masters of the refinements of taxation ; but they have ever beeu ignorant of those means which have* constituted the foundation of the material success of Western civilization in the old world and the new.

The allusion which has just been made to the Public Works Loan raised in India in 1855, leads to the remark, that the way in which the notifications of this and other Indian Debts of the Presidencies have been gazetted, as well as the Forms in which they have been issued, justify these three inferences:—

(1). That the public territorial debts, nominally assigned to separate Presidencies of India, are liot distinct chargeS upon the security of the Revenues of the single Presidency only.

(2). That the Revenues of one Presidency are not primarily liable, nor those of all or any of the other Presidencies only secondarily liable, but each guarantees the rest.

(3). That if all Revenue were lost from any one Presidency, or in other words, if we relinquished the possession of its territory, the liability under the debt would devolve upon the other Presidencies, and in such event, would still have to be discharged'to the creditors generally.

These are substantially centralized, as opposed to localized, conditions of Finance; but, with all due deference t6 those who are better qualified to form a right judgment on the special applicability of such a system to Public Works'Loans in India, I am inclined to doubt its expediency or advantage. It appears to me that it would not only be more equitable, hut that it would promote infinitely more of native co-operation, if the security were, restricted either to separate Presidencies, or to separate large Districts or Collectorates, instead of extending it to the whole of the Indian Revenues;—the result would be, a more effectual enlistment of local and native knowledge, interests, and sympathies in useful and profitable public

▪works.   Colonization, whether by Europeans or by natives of India,* of select and healthy regions adapted for the growth of particular products, might also be very materially facilitated through the medium of such a beneficial interest in financial improvement.

One of the lessons of an experience which our country has gained in India, after a deplorable sacrifice of the brave life and heroic virtue of some of the noblest of its children, is, that military occupation alone can never retain its possession.   It must be seconded by more active progress in developing the resources of the sod, under the direction of the British, but conjointly with, and chiefly through ı the better employment of, the labour of the native population. Whilst a -wise economy is undoubtedly a great desideratum in India, as elsewhere, nevertheless its opposite 'extreme, a parsimonious policy", would sooner perhaps than in any other part of the world, destroy every prospect of the wished-for progress.

III.—*Fiscal conditions that regulate Indian Finance, compared with, those applicable to Sritish Finance.*

Consideration of historical evidence is essential to any due appreciation of fiscal systems in those countries of Europe where precedent and ancient institutions flourish.   This may seem a truism, but such an pbjection may be borne with, as it will serve to place in stronger relief the circumstance that the same course must even more fully apply to any investigation of the rationale of the Indian fiscal system, in wjiich the memory of ages gone by is the reality of to-day.   The Hindoo, bred in th^ same debasing idolatries as his ancestors, and the Mussulman, shackled with the iutoleraucies and infallibility of his law, are always looking back from the British ceiituiy of power to an antecedent state of things; their minds are loth to grasp the idea of progress and change.

The more our Indian fellow-subjects study their own annalists and historians, the deeper are they imbued with ide'.,s unfitted for the present day.   They drink at a poisoned source, which exalts the principle of the exploitation of the many for the good of the few; the glitter, pomp, and show of the ruler and his satellites, at the expense of the grinding poverty and starvation of the subject.   They naturally recur to the most striking example of administrative eclat which their records present.   They point with some pride to the rule of Akbar, whose dominion was greatly more extensive, and

---

* The number of *Europeans* in the service of the East India Company in the three Presidencies of Bengal, Bombay, and Madras, did not amount to more than about 40,000 in the year 1851.   This included nomen and children.   The total divided as to sex gives about 29,000 males and 11,000 females.   The number of Europeans not in the service of the East India Company does not appear to have been returned to the English Census Commission of 1851.   Its total is believed to be very small.

whose revenue was some forty or fifty times larger, than that of his contemporary, Queen Elizabeth; but they are slow to perceive that even the wisdom of an Akbar failed to lay the foimdations of methods which could permanently conduce to the wealth and well-being of the people. '

' The revised Land Assessment of Akbar and his finance ministers, Tuder Mull and Mozuffer Khan, the formation of which dates from A.D. 1578 and 1579, errs against the just principles of the proportionality of Taxation. It was an attempt to lay the whole burden of taxation on the Land, and to nemit the other sources of revenue fromi indirect and direct taxation levied under the authority of the Mahomedan law. There is no satisfactory evidence that it was successfully applied, in practice, even in Akbar's reign, or. that the Taxes said to have been remitted were positively not exacted. This much appears certain, that they soon had to be reverted to. Whether, however, a system of taxation be eclectic like Akbar's, or general and regulated so as to fall bn all descriptions of property, its result under native rule, ready to gather without planting, and to reap without sowing, neglecting to promote industry and energy among the people, or to allow them to recover from perpetual and harassing exactions, was inevitably one of collapse. This method of taxing may be compared with a chronic habit of bleeding, without leaving breathing time, or „ affording rest and nourishment.

Under an impoverishing condition of aggressive, despotic, and civil wars, the eclectic system of raising an undue proportion of revenue from direct sources wan as prejudicial as would have been exclusive indirect taxation. A due admixture of both methods is the only one which could provide for a lengthened period against the exhaustion from such a drain on productive resources.

It is by no means uninteresting to compare Uie ancient Indian and English svstems of taxation. It is here proposed to give some brief remarks <?n the somewhat remarkable parallelisms which may be traced between them; these are arranged in the following Tabular statement.

The leading source of information on the Mahomedan system of Eevenue and Taxation in India is the ATKEN AKBABEE, or Institutes of Akbar. Erom notes on English versions of the portion of that work which relates to these branches of administration, the first column of the next TABLE, H, has been compiled. Its first eleven items (under the letter A) show the Taxes in chief under the general jjrovisions and basis of the Mahomedan law in vigour in India from the commencement of the Eleventh Century. The next thirty items (under the letter B) show some of the principal of the Taxes of a subsidiary kind, which were generally and simultaneously imposed. The latter, and other analogous imposts, aje said to have been repealed by' Akbar, but succeeding sovereigns were obliged to re-iinpose them to make up their revenues. Akbar is also asserted to have repealed the majority of the more important taxes first above referred to, particularly the Poll-Tax, which, obnoxious and opposed as it was to the feelings of the people, was nevertheless immensely productive.

In the second column of the Table, the Indian nomenclature of the Taxes is given, chiefly upon the authority of the author of " Observations on the Law and Constitution of India." (London, 1825,)

In the third column are appended some brief notes on the parallelism which it appears to me mayc.be drawn between the fiscal systems of India and England; and these may, perhaps, be found sufficient- to indicate, that in ingenuity and expansiveness of plan, the Tax collectors of the East have always been fuUy up to the mark of their brethren in the Weat, and in many respects have surpassed them.

TABLE H.

PABAILEUSMS *of the* INMAN *and* ENGLISH SVSTEMS *of* REVENUE *and* TAXATION.

1	S	S
INDIAN TAXES.	*Indian Nomenclaiurf.*	**Notes and Remarks on TAXES** of a precisely similar, nr nearly analogous,nature in ENGLAND-
(A.>—TAXES IN CHPEF *Under the general provisione and baeie of the Ufahomedan haw.*		
u TITRES, commuted into T-and-Tax (fioe il0» 21.), as the Mahomedan law does not permit Tithes as well as Land-Tax to bo levied on the same Land	Ooshr b	Tithes.
n. LAND-TAX.- ' '"v.	Kliuraiy	Land'Tax.
HI. TBIBUTB . ,		Tributes from Scotland, &c., swelled the Revenue of England In medimval times. In modem days it indirectly derives some benefit firom Indian Tribute.
nr. CUSTOMS	Ooshr-oot tujourut	Customs.
T. CATTLE TAX on Camels, oxen, she^, and goats	Zukaut .	*A* Poll-Tax on Sbcq> was levied in Í England by tlie 8 de 4 Edw. VI, 1649: repealed in followingyear.
Ti. PBOPEBTT TAX of Per Cent OU Gold and Silver bullion, Coin, ornaments, and Plate. PBOPBBTV AND INCOMS TAX, *Zj* per Cent-, *ad valorem,* on Stock in Trade, and on Profits derived from any kind of moveable or personal property	Zukaut	Property Taxes on Gold and Silver Bullion, Coin, &c., can be traced in England from the time of Henry II (A.D. 1188), and, through tlie medium of the Land-Tax Assessment, down to the period of tlie Commonwealth. Income Taxes on S(ock-in-Trado, and on Profits therefrom, and Oom personal property generally. Oom the same date (1188), and even previously, down to the present time*

TAOLU H.—Co«/f»«c4* '

1			S

IXOIAH TA3(ES.	*Indian ^fomcncliitHrc,'*	Not^ and Uomarlcs Dn TAxifs of n precisely similar^ or nearly analogous, nature inExOLAM*.

vit. POOR RATES. Aims for Abe relief of die poor, including expiutoiy Mivoflerings, and .votivo-oflurings. Tiio xVbnsivcrcpayable on tba<-rd or fotivni of .*Mr, soon* alter the jZ»o *marautt, or* Alaluurlctlan *Lont, but only by Moslems .o.f age, male and female, who, besides boUso, funii-^ turo, *iic.,* and. Ip.bouring slaves, p(»sscs.sc(1 200 Dirlmms of property. .TFaking the DlrhumatO^., this rqiresontcddicsuin uf«t»ISs.) — StiAtikiiVoid fcU — A'distinct purnllelism is to be-ilrawn- ..for .the. period previous to Ute fiefbrUiutiott iu the u/Tcrings (o snrijie>un<l altars, ami Ilteemlow* menu of cburch<*3 and tnonns* Usriqs. wliicb dtspeused aims to the Ppiq*. , Atlor the Monastorios and Itoligioas^iouses wero'Suppressed >ve have the Purlinmenlai^*)egis« . latinii of 43 Elizabeth, c. 2, (he ■Toinidtttion of our Eng)t^i pbor

viit. Pott TAX. From the u'oaltby, or owners of from lOiOOO'to ld^OOO Dirbtims of property, t. e., of from 30dZ. to 5031., 48 Dirbnms per annum (t. e.. about 38s.) From the inidillo classes, possessed of pro-; pcrty» but not indopOndent, 24 Dir»bums (i.e., 10*-) per annum. And from Alic labouring, classes, 12 Dir--'buins (i. e.. Os. (kZ.), payable by niontbly instalments of 1 Dirbnm 'I'bis Poll, or Capitation Tux, -was unpopular in India, ohen repeated and revived, and Gnally *l done away widi in 1745. — Jixomdj — Poll Taxes, sometimes at a uniform n^te,. an<l nt other times on a scale, occording .br wealth *. .or .dignity, were levied,.io tlicfoce o.f nm.ci) opposition, os for back os by sovereigns of die Plontn< genet lino: Tlie Parlininonis of li^onry VHl and- Clmrl^ *t-* revived (lie Tax 'temporarily, and, with better success in its collection. .*llie Jost revival was-in die* ,reign of William and Mary,.when* it.oxpifcd .iu die midst of general unpopularity and discontent at its ineidelice.

I.X.. RoYAhTYi on War Prizes or Flumlor, Mining- Produce, Treasure Trove, and Wrecks Tins was termed FiAhs," such being (no Sovereign's share.accord!ng to the Koran. — Kbuonu -ft — War Prizes, Ransoms, and Plunder, Minifig Royalties, Treasure Trove, and- Wrecks, belonged, iu *eliiof* measure, to Englum sovorcigns-froro tile earliest times, but tlieir sliaro 'yas greater lhaq onc-niUi. in theory Alley were ondded to all.

X. ESCHEATS ;pn'tporiy falling to the crown, in delault of legal boirs, or by confiscation Gir ditrereuce of re« ligion, barrinuJiihoritonco if etthor party tlieroto ue *a* Moslem^ — Feudal escheat* in England from Saxpij^and Norman times down to die ab'jb'lioii of *tiia Court o C* M'arefs and Livorie.s, *temp. Charles II* Since dien escheats from failure of lleirs only.

XL WsK TAXES — The only special War Taxes in England, called Boncvolo»ce.s, were at drst assumed to Ito volun* ta^, but soon became obligatory e.xaoiions.

9

(B.)>0^UDStDIARY TAXES *levied by the Mahomedan Suvereigne.*

1. 7*ax OU Marriages, by a variable scale, according to the woahh and position of the poronts, varying from 20 molnirs to 2 dams. — For about ten years, commencing from iGOd.a hlarriago Tax existed in England. U'lle feudal rights to Fines on Marriages may also be rofurrird to.

2. Succession or Inlroduction'Tnxos — Posh kUsh .... — Court Fees on Installation, acccs* siou to Peerage, Asc.

3. Port Duties, Admiralty duos .... — Moor buhree ,. Kurccaee — Port and Admiralty Dues.

4', Tax on convocations assembled to sottlo busiuoss, and levied on each ' person; '"

TABLE **H.**—*Continued.*

I	2	s
INDIAN TAXES.	*Indian Nomenclature,*	Notes and Remarks on TAXES of a precisely similar^ or nearly analogous,nature in ENGLAND.
5. Tux on oxen ...♦	Gaoshiimaree..	
6. „ „ Fruit-trees	Sire deruktee..	
7. „ „ Artizaiis..	Fiirook Aksam peshoh	
8- „ „ Sale of Cattle		
9. Market Dues	Hasile bazar ..	
10. Tax on hemp, blankets, ghee or Oil, raw hides		
11. Tax on measuring land...............		
12. „ „ weighing.............................		Stamp (Ml weights and scales.
13. „ for killing cultle......................		
14. „ on tanning		
16. „ „ gambling with dice		Stamp duties on dice.
16. „ „ sawing timber............. ..		
17. ı „ „ Transit passports.................	Kabdaree	
18. Hearth Money		Hearth Money.
19. .Tax on Buyer and Seller of Houses		Auctioneer s license.
20. Tax on Salt made from earth...•		Salt Tax finally repealed in England iu 1825.
21. „ „ the commencement of reaping	Rilkutty	
22. Tax on Lime for building...........		
23. „ ℘ Spirituous liquors		Excise on Spirits.
24. ℓℓ » Brokerage		Transfer Stamps.
25. ℓℓ Fishermen		
26. ℘ n Mint Taxes		Seignorage on coinage of Gold from a very early period in England, discontinued in 1666, continued on Silver and Copper coin.
o		
2T. „ „ Coin or Bullion Dealers.	Snrranfee ᵞ*	
28. Tax lbr Police officers	Darogimnee	Police Rates.
20. „ „ Under-collectors. .	'I'tssceldaree	
30. „ „ Money-triers.....................	Fotahdoree..	

The preceding long catalogue of Taxes does not nierely represent an ancient state of things which has become obsolete.   On the contrary, it is almost unchanged at the present time, in*ᵗ those parts of Hindostan where Native rule still continues.   It rather falls short of, than over estimates, the subtle ramifications of the fiscal system there prevalent.   As examples in point, it is interesting to observe what were the facts in the two comparatively recent annexations of the Punjab and Sinde.   *

As regards the PUNJAB, reference may with advantage be made •to a remarkable Document which has deservedly reflected much honour on the distinguished Administration of whose talents and public spirit it wiU be an enduring monument.   The allusion here is to the " General Report on the Administration of the Punjab for the years 1849-50 and 1850-51."   (Printed for the Court of Directors of the East India Company: London, 1854).   In referring to the system of Taxation under the ruler who had immediately preceded the English, and whose ɩ territory was. finally annexed in the spring of 1849, Sir Henry Lawrence, Mr. John Lawrence, and Mr. Robert Montgomery state (see paragraph 299):—

" Under Runjeet Sing the whole country was threaded with a net work of preventive lines.

" These lines were dotted with innumerable posts for the collection of every kind of tax, direct and indirect. At the same set of stations, excise and customstaxes', town-dues, transit-duties, capitation-imposts, artisan-fees, were all levied. The principle was to extract taxation from everything indiscriminately. No distinction was made between domestic and foreign industry, between articles of indigenous and extraneous production, between manufactures at home and abroad. The artisans of Lahore and Umritsur were taxed, together with the goldsmiths and ironmongers of Cabul; the silks of Mooltan and the cloths of the Punjab were no less dutiable than the cotton goods of Europe; the shawls of Cashmere, the groceries of Cabul, the dried fruits of Central Asia. The cotton, indigo and sugar of the Punjab, had to pay an excise about equal in amount to the customs levied on the same produce imported from Hindostan. * Nor was salt the only necessary of life subject to taxation; ghee, tobacco, vegetables, all the poor men's luxuries, were placed under contribution."

The above quotation is shortened to make room for the following passage in the context, which is of importance and interest as showing that a thorough system of mixed direct and indirect Taxation is an effectual preservative from a disturbance of the proportionality and equity of Taxation (see paragraph 300);

" But, on the whole, the taxation could not be called uneven, inasmuch as it embraced everything; every class from the richest to tWte poorest, every locality, every thoroughfare, every town "and willage, every article, wherever sold, imported or exported, domestic or foreign. 'That such a multiform system of taxation did not harass the people, fetter trade, and produce oppression, can scarcely be supposed; but still commerce did somehow thrive, and a sturdy people grew and multiplied to a degree which, under such disadvantages, European political economists would have thought hardly possible." •

With revpect to SINDE, it will be convenient to arrange, in the following TABLE J, a list of the Taxes repealed soon after that country was conquered. The original materials will be found in the Return to Order of the House of Lords (l63/'53). We need only here remark, that many of the Items can be traced to their counterparts in the TABLE H which we have just now been considering.

It is particularly to be observed that direct taxation by native governments in the form of Income and Property Taxes, prevailed from time immemorial; and there is no doubt that such taxes were imposed long before the Mahomedan period by the Hindoo Code of Menu.'* Direct Taxation by Income and Property Tax has, however, been abolished by the British Administration in India. This 'will be further referred to in the next part of these remarks.

* Bee, *post,* tinder bead of (4) MOTURPHA, in the fourth section of this paper.

TABLE J.

Descriptive Statement of Xss,s& BEFEAEED IN SINDB   the Governorship of the late Sir Charles Napier, from, 1843 to 1846.

Description of TAX.

1. Rabadaree *or* Transit Duty
2. Ta.x levied on Goods exported and imported within the Province. (Land Customs).
3. Cbowth Shurafee; Tax levied from Shroffs on account of Excliange of -Coius or Goldsmiths' Contract
4. Mochee Poorah; Tax levied from Tunners of Lather or Tannery Contract
5. Zar Cohee ; Tax levied from Manu-' factures of Gold Leaf, or Arsiduc Contract
6. Kinnra; Tax levied on a kind pf Red Colour manufactured from the Bark of a Tree
7. Keermeex Tax; a Tax on Cochineal
8.' Duin; Tax on Curds
9. " Dulalce ' Tobacco}" Tax levied from Brokers dealing in Tobacco
JO. Damn Teeratb; a Tax levied from Pilgrims proceeding to the annual Fair at the Hot Spring at Lackie
11. Dbur Tbaraxoo; Tax levied from certain privileged Gmin Measurers existent in all principal Cities, where all the Graia imported was measured by them alone, in con-sideration of which Privilege they levied a certain Fee from the Importers
12. Bhayath and Meer Imarath; Tax levied on Fruits produced in Gar-dens, and the latter on Houses and Building Materials sold
13. Kirmith; Tax levied on Sweetmeats made of Sugar, during the Hindoo Festival of Dewallee
14. Tax on the Marriage of the Poorer Classes
15. Tax on Carpenters

Deacription of TAX.

16. Puoacherree or Grazing j Tax levied on the Muncher Lake
17. Tlinl Burath; Tax from klussulmen on their Festivals
18.   ChoongeeFee on Grain at Sehwan
19. Cnickendose; Tax upon Silk Em-broiderers
20. Tufed baf; Tax levied on Cotton Fabric Manufacturers
21. Tax levied on Ivory Manufacturers or Turners
22. Ruin Saz; Tax levied from Brasiers
23. Nidaff; Tax levied from Cotton Cleaners
24. Coombar; Tax levied from Potters
25. Sonar; Tax levied from Gold and Silver Smiths
26. Paish Cush .and Sheu Soomaree ; Poll Tax
27. Tax levied on Butchers
28.   on Corn Grinders
29.   »   on 'Vegetable Sellers
30.   from Shopkeepers
31.   „   on Oil Manufacturers
32.   on Fish-sellers
33. Moree; Tax levied on Boats anchor-ing at any Port in the River.
34. Russoom Canagholl; Tax on Goods transported to any Place, inde-pendent of the Levy of the Cus-toms Duties
35. " DoorkaneeTax levied on tlie opening of new Doors and Win-dows of Shops
36. " Puim j" Tax on Ipishcs for mak-ing Mats
37. •' Nurruck Rogun   Tax levied when the Rate of Ghee was high in the Market
38. Atbusbazee; Taxes on the Makers of Fireworks

There remain to be noticed some of the distinguishing features as respects the origin and incidence of the Indian Land-Tax.

A century has not yet elapsed since the East India Company became sovereign landlords and collectors of revenue on their inde-pendent account; when Bengal, Behar, and Orissa'were ceded to them, and the donor called the gift the " paradise of the world." What may be termed the modern System of Revenue was inaugurated under the government of Lord Cornwallis.   In 1793 was passed the first of a series of regulations and acts which have heeu continued to the present time by a rapid succession of amendments and reforms. Previously, and dating from the adiuiuistratiou of Clive, efforts had been made in the same direction. .That period was, however, one attended with the difficulties of an experimental, or provisional, kind of legislation, and with the pre-occupations of military events.

Between 1772 and 1793, four Committees of the House of Commons deliberated on Indian affairs—the memorable administration of Warren Hastings had taken its place in history—the Board of Con-, trol had been instituted. *

In the interval different Land Bevenue systems had been tried. Annual, quinquennial, and decennial, settlements were tested; but no radical change of the plans of native rulers had been essayed. In the pursuit of revenue, much of the oppression and exaction of those rulers had been continuedi. These characteristics were not simply the results of the decline of the Mogul empire. In the Hindoo, as well as in 'the Mahomedan, system, may be traced the origin, common to all great empires, of the military conqueror parcelling out the possession of the land, retaining a share of the produce for himself and his immediate followers, and distributing grants Eent-Free, or subject to conditions, more or less onerous, of special tenure.

Both the Hindoo and Mahomedan plans seem to have proceeded upon the sovereign's share being calculated on^ the gross produce, and not on the net produce or rent remaining after the expenses of cultivation are deducted. The Hindoo belief was, that in remote antiquity the earth became, by conquest, the property of the holy Parasa Hama. That this individual, or Demi-god, presented the earth in free gift to the sage Casyapa, who, in his turn, committed it to the soldier-tribe or caste of the Cshatriyas, because of their protective powers. That from them it passed into the proprietorship of successive conquerors, and not into that of the cultivators or snbjects- But the latter might acquire property by payment of annual rent, or rent for terms of years. If thia rent was not paid, the contract was annulled. And, where there was no special agreement, a bidder for the land at a higher rent could oust the actual holder at the expiry of the annual, or terra, tenancy. And by rent a given proportion of produce, and not a specific amount of money, was implied. Theoretically* the Hindoo sovereign's legal proportion was one-sLxth in ordinary time, and one-fourth in War time. But it is not to be supposed that the Hindoo rulers of ancient days were a whit bitter,, or more lenient, than their Moslem successors, who soon extended

---

* See **works; the late Professor *Jones* of Haileybury's unfinished Treatise on Rentt &c.**

the proportion to one-third from lands of the usual class, and to one-half from lands naturally irrigated by flood rivers.

The rule, of conquest conferring proprietorship, was preserved, in the fullest integrityj by the Mahomedan code. The theory and practice of its operation are very clearly defined in the following extract from the anonymous work entitled " Obsenations on the Law and Constitution of India, &c.," (London, 1825), which has been before referred to. The author states (p. 97):

" By the Moohummudan revenue lan s a distinction is made between the *Moslem* and the *Zimmee,* or non-Moslem subject, to which it is necessary to attend. This distinction is great with respect to the land revenue; but it is applicable, only, to the land of *Arabia Proper,* and to conquered provinces, when the lands are divided amongst the conquerors. Thus the Moslem pays the *OosAr,* or tithe of his crop; the Zimmee, the heavier impost of *Khurauj,* which by law may amount to, but cannot exceed, half the produce, t. e., five tithes. But, on the other band, the . Moslem is liable to several annual and occasional taxes, from which the Zimmee is exempt, amounting to about two or three per rent, of his property (not'of the produce merely), under the name of *SndnttaK* and *ZVlSoKl,* or pious benevolences. 1 use this word because the English reader will recognise it.

" But as India was conquered by force of arms, ard the inhabitants were sufiered to remain in it, and their lands were restored to them on paying the capitation tax and the *Klmrauj,* or land revenue, by law the whole land of India is Khuraujee land, the Hindoo and other inhabitants, uubelievers, are Zimmee, and tte land is liable to the Khurauj, whether it be in possession of a Moslem or a Zimmee. This is the law of Moohummudan conquest; and the fact corresponds with the law. By law the *Ooshr* and *Khurauj* cannot both be exacted from the same land; consequently, in India, tlie land revenue, payable by a Moslem and a Zimmee, by law, would be the same, and *io defacto* it was."

Proprietary right of the state to the reut; and possessory, but subsidiary, right of the subject to the land; were thus clearly defined by the Mahomedan law. In every ordinary sense of the term, the chief landlord was the State. And the British government holds that position in India by the same rule of conquest which has prevailed there from time immemorial in the Mahomedan ,4ind Hindoo dynasties. The parallel as to origin and pi-inciple of such a right is so complete with that of the feudal tenures and land-taxes, of Europe, and of England in particular, that we may merely restrict our notice to the fact.

We now pass to a point of practical importance, viz.: LAND-TAX REDEMPTION SO far as applicable to INDIA.

The plan of rendering the Land-Tax permanent in amount, was adopted by statute in India, about four years before it was so in Great Britain. It is true that in this country a given maximum never had been exceeded in the Acts passed from year to year since the time of William and Mary, but permanent legislation did not take place until Mr. Pitt's Act was passed in 1797; whilst, in Bengal, the Marquis of Cornwallis had carried into effect his Pernia-

nent Settlement, in 1793. But there is a highly important distinction to be remarked, rendering the analogy less substantial than
would at first appear. Mr. Pitt introduced his Land-Tax measure,
in order to render perpetual a legal claim of the State to a obtain
reserved rent, of customary fixed amount, nnd which constituted at
the time no more than about *Ten* per cent, of the British Revenue.*
Lord'Cornwallis introduced his Land-Tax measure, in order to render
perpetu!il a legal claim of the East Indian government to a reserved
rent, which had not, by custom, been of fixed amount, and which
constituted at the time as much as *Fifty-six* per cent, of the whole
Bengal Revenue.   •

There was a difference, therefore, both in the circumstance of the
customary fixity of amount in the one instance, as compared with
its indeterminateness in the other; and in the circumstance of the
far greater comparative moment of such a step as a permanent
renunciation, in India, of the power of increasing rent, which
there formed the lending item of revenue. In the United Kingdom, the equilibrium and proportionality of taxation, has, all
things considered, usually been as well adjusted as could reason-
ably be expected; and Mr. Pitt's financial discernment was
never more conspicuous than in his promotion of a mixed system
of direct and indirect taxation as the moat efficient aid to such an
adjustment. In India, owing partly to its inferior civilization preventing representative government, re-adjustment of methods of taxa-
. tion is more difficult and more experimental.

And, if these grounds have weight, they cdttainly lend force to
the conclusion that the permSnent settlement of the Government
Rent, or Land Tax in the lower provinces of Bengal, was an improvi-
dent and unwise measure. That the motive of its institution was
upright and well-intentioned is not doubted, but it is a branch of the
question which does not belong to the present line of inquiry. Eor-
tunately, too^the measure is limited to the comparatively narrow area
to which it was applied at the outset. The Statistics in the first part
of this paper will enable some idea to be formed of its size and population, contrasted with the rest of British India; and the reader will
judge whether an extravagant amount of controversial literature has
not been wasted in India, and in this country, upon the debateable
points of conditions that apply to a section of the community of India,
which, owing to the annexations of territory that have gone on
(almost continuously) during the lifetime of the present generation,
has ceased to possess the nearly exclusive importance it once had.

By this, it is not meant to be contended that the Lower Pro-

---

* In estimating this proportion, it has been considered right to take the ordinary
revenue of Great Britain in 1797, *exclusive* of all receipts from Loans. If the latter
were included, the proportion would be reduced from 10 to about 5 per cent.

A'inces of Bengal have not the fullest title-to the warm interest and attention which the Indian administration direct towards them. Far from such a view—The progress and condition of their population are Jjound up with the earliest associations of British rule,—and all that the preceding rercatks are intended to convey, is, that the time and debate that used formerly to be bestowed upon the permanent settlement of Bengal, in arguments for and against it, can at the present day be more profitably directed to the consideration of other matters,- upon which a right judgment really affects the welfare of the people of the whole of India. The permanent settlement of the Land Bevenue, so far as regards a part- of & Presidency, and amongst a portion of these people, is an established fact; and this can never be disturbed without breach of faith such as we refuse, as Ehglishmen, even to entertain.

There is a single useful question branching out of this subject,' namely:—*How the conditions of the Permanent Settlement can host ihe utilized?*

Acting upon the precedent of the principle of Mr. Pitt's, measure, which rendered the permanent British Land Tax redeemable, a similar course has sometimes been suggested for India. Upon, the maturest reflection I have been able to give to the principles involved iu those methods of redemption, (which however inefficiently, were -described with some pains in niy paper on British Land Tax, in- •serted in the last volume of the Society's Transactions), it appoiirs to me that the extension of too wide a generalization of a Eedemption of the Laud Tax would be as wrong as, and far less excusable than, the permanent settlement itself. If, however, the carrying out of such a suggestion were restricted in its field of operation distinctly to Bengal alone, or rather, to those portions of the Bengal Presidency wtiere the Permanent Settlement is an existing institution of the 'country and cannofe-be reversed, there do not appear any valid objections to a Land Tax Eedemption being effectually carrigd out.

The method should be a cancelment of Land Tax in exchange for 'a transfer and cancelment of such an amount of nominal capital in the Indian Public Debt, as produces an annual dividend precisely equal to the Land Tax redeemed.

At 5 Per Cent. Interest, each Million of Land Tax so redeemed in exchange for its equivalent in Indian Stock, would pay off Twenty ■Millions of the Debt, or at $4^$ Per Cent. Interest, 22,222,000/. would be similarly paid off.

A redemption'of about Sixty-two Per Cent, of the Bengal Land Tax, say of 2,916,000/., out of 4,688,000/. (its aggregate amount as in 1855-6), would pay off the *whole* of the existing Public Debt of the East India'Company charged on the Eevenues of India, which, as already shown, amounted (exclusive of the Capital Stock, but inelusive of the 8,000,000?. of Loan to be raised for the Mutiny Expenses) to the Sum of 68,434,000?., on 1st May, 1858.

A redemption of this kind, not obligatory, but purely permissive, and to be acted upon at the Landholder's own wish, and when his means admitted, would be gradual and self-adjusting; but probably neither the requisite funds, nor the inclination to redeem, would be found wanting in Bengal.

The operation is one of balance or interchange of two equivalents. Instead of the British government in India paying with one hand to the Stockholders of the Debt about 2,916,000?. of annual interest, and receiving with the other hand from the Bengal Landholders about 4| Millions of annual Land Tax, it would eventually write off 2,916,000?. of Land Tax, and the whole amount of the existing Indian Debt would be cancelled. .

It must, however, be observed, that os.the rate of interest on the existing nominal capital of the Indian Debt is 4| per cent., any possible advantage from some future reduction of Interest would be prevented from accruing. As this is a deferred contingency, its pecuniary effect upon the final result of a Redemption measure is not of much importance. On the other side, it should be noticed that the immediate expenses of collecting the Land Tax in Beng^ are 6 Per Cent., or about 175,000?. per annum on the portion of that tax represented by the sum of 2,916,000?. just referred to; and these expenses would be entirely saved by the Kedemption. The cost of administering the Debt, or in other words, the management' expenses of paying Dividends of 2,910,00Q?., would also be saved.

But the whole measure of the good it would accomplish is not to be expressed in the mere money result. The middleman, and the inferior servants and agents who are said to oppress the Bengal Eyot, would be more restrained from the power of exercising their love of exaction. , And where the state receives, as in Bengal, so large a portion of thuiBent of the soil, and can disburden itself of the position of chief landlord without any sacrifice, as it would there be enabled to do, it is highly politic thus to increase the number of its freeholding subjects, and at the same time to limit their opportunities of oppressing the poorer and harder-working classes. The wealth of the country would be much promoted by the formation of an independent middle class; industrial enterprise would have a bettor chance of success; a larger revenue from taxation, whether indirectly or directly, would be easier met; European imports would increase; the execution of productive public works would be facilitated; and benefits of the utmost moment to the people of India, and to this country, would be the sure result.

ly.—*Facts and Statistics tearing upon the past 'history and progress of Ftevenue and Taxation in British India, during the sixty-four years 1792-93 to 1855-56.*

The progress of the Eevenue of India is a subject which cannot be reviewed, even in a general manner, except, the inquirer be content to face considerable labour in analyzing and condensing particulars interspersed in a great variety of financial statements. As some evidence of the extent of the surface to be gone over in any complete review of them, it may be noticed thatj for one year only, the volume of accounts of territorial revenue and disbursement, as now presented to Parliament, occupies some seventy folios. The Home Eeturns (presented annually under the same Act of Parliament, 3 & 4 Vm. IV, c. 85) take up.about twelve folios. Most of the Eeturns are' comprehensive and well arranged, and the fifty, or thereabout, of -separate. statements contained in the first or Indian volume of returns, not only-include the audited or passed accounts of the particular year to which the volume specially applies, but also an estimate for the succeeding year, and.comparative statements respecting these two years in juxtaposition with the figures for the two previous years.

In so extensive a government it has not hitherto been found possible to get in and print the final accounts until the lapse of a longer time than might be wished. Por instance, at the present time (April, 1858), the Ijist Eetum printed is that for the financial year 1855-56, that is, ended 30th April, 1856, so that in practice no final statement is before the public which is not about 2 years in arrear or say nearly $2^\wedge$ years old; and it follows, that the provisional estimates are one yeap, or more nearly, IJ year old.

Whilst the annual returns just indicated are pre-eminently the source of information as to the finances of any particular year, the student who has regard to the necessity for economizirg his time and labour, in the collection of data to enable him to arrive at a broad and general view of the progress of the several branches of Indian Eevenue, will accomplish that object to some extent by making use of the Eevenue Statistics contained in the House of Commons Papers 836/55 and 16/57.* In these papers are given the figures of each head of- Taxation, in each Presidency, since 1792. The amounts are stated throughout in Pounds Sterling, at the uniform rate of Two Shillings the Company's Eupee. The Gross annual receipts show an

---

* The first-mentioned paper is under the tide of '• Land Tax (East India)." Returns to Mr. Blackett's motion. Ordered to be printed 22nd June, 1855.—The other paper is under the title of " East India (Revenue)." Return to Mr. Arthur Mills's motion, in continuation of the above. Ordered to be printed 11th December, 1857.

excess over the annual Parliamentary returns from the year 1836-7, owing partly to this method of converting the revenue into sterling, and further, by the deduction in a different manner in the Parliamentary accounts, of the cost of collecting the revenue.

The Statistics contained ih the returns here referred to, would take up at least Forty Pages of the size of the Statistical Journal to reprint in full, and even then we should only have before us the undigested material. For the purposes of the present paper, it has been deemed desirable to re-arrange thia collection of materials into periods of five years each, to calcula^ the *annzial* average Eevenue during each period, and also the Batio of each branch to the total Eevenue raised. By this means a connected and condensed review of the whole progress of the Eevenue, during twelve quinquennial periods, and one period of four years, down to the date of the latest accounts, can be seen in the columns of the following TABLES K and L. These are arranged in chronological order, and the latter of the two, viz, TABLE L, contains a synopsis of the average *annual* revenue derived from all sources, with the per-centages of each branch (1) in the period of four years just referred to; (2) in the preceding period of sixty years; and .(3) in the aggregate whole period of sixty-four years.

Following these Tables is another Table (M), giving a summary of the aggregate total amounts of the separate branches of revenue during the whole period. This Table also explains, in the column headed "Eemarks," the reasons for some Items of revenue appearing in certain periods and not in otjiers, or in other words, the dates of the introduction or repeal of those items of revenue or taxation in different parts of India.

The construction of these three Tables, K, L, and M, has demanded considerable labour; but, it is submitted, this can scarcely be said to have been uselessly expended, as the Tables give such a condensed view of the many details of the Indian Eevenue during a prolonged period of time, as is not elsewhere obtainable.

In the first part of the present paper it will have been noticed that the Items of revenue are given for the five governments of India separately. To have preserved this separation in the figures which here follow, would have extended the statement to an inconvenient length, and rendered it less clear; besides which, it is not possible to arrive at a definite statistical view of the exact rate of increase of the territorial limits, and of the population, of the several divisions of India, during past periods of annexation and rapid growth.

It is, perhaps, necessary to repeat, that throughout the tables three 0's (000) are omitted at the unit end of each amount of revenue. Thus, in the second column of the immediately following TABLE K, the Land Eevenue for India in the five years 1792--3 to

s S

1796-7,18 expressed as having averaged 4,068 Millions Sterling.   This must he read 4,068,0001.; and 0 264 as the Opium Eevenue given in the next line but one, must be read 264,0001.

TABLE K.

ATERAOB *Annual* EEVENUE *derived from all'Sources, with* PER CENTAOR PROPORTIONS *of the Total of each Branch, as raised in the* WHOLE *of* INDIA *in* TWELVE SEPARATE PERIODS OF FIVE YEARS EACH *during the Sixty Years* 1792-1852.

1	3	3	4	6	6	7
	Five Years, 1792-3 to 179G-7.		Five Years, 1797-8 to 1801-2.		Five Years, 1802-3 to 1806-7.	
Bnuiehes of Revenue,	Average Revenue.	Ratio of each Branch to Total Revenue.	Average *Jnnttal* Revenue.	Ratto of each Branch to Total Revenue.	Average *Alnnual* Revenue.	Ratio of each Branchto Total Revenue.
	Mlns. £	per Cent.	Mlns. £	Per Cent	Mlns.	Percent.
1. Land	4-068	5c'J3	4-126	42'oz	4-582	31-99
5. Salt	1-207	14'93	1-188	12*10	1-589	11*09
6. Opium	0-264	3'-t7	0-312	3-18	0-579	4-04
7. Post Office	0-028	•35	0-042	•43	0-048	•34
8.			0-030.	•30	0-062	'43
9. Customs	0-192	2'38	0-304	3-10	0-596	4.-16
10. Mint	0'008	'IO	0-0U8	'08	0-012	•08
12. Miscellaneous	2-315	t8-6+	3-809	38-79	6-857	47-87
Total Avg. Revenue	8-o8i	X00'	9'819	l00*	«4'325	l00*
Total Avg. Charges	6-900	85'4	10-197	103-8	15-554	io8-6
Average Indian Surplus	1-182					
Average Indian Defi-l ciency ....(					1-229	

TABLE K.—*Continued.*

1	*a* 3	4	6	6	*1*
	Five Years, 1807-8 to 1811-12.		Five Years, 1812-13 to 1816-17.		Five Years, 1817>18to1821-2.
Branches Tof Revenue.	Average *Annual* Revenue.	Ratio of each Branch to Total Revenue.	Average -sfnnMU Revenue.	Ratio of each Branch to Total Revenue.	Average Revenue.	Ratio of each Branch to Total Revenue.

	Mlns. £	Per Cent.	Mlns. 26	Per Cent.	Mlns. £	Percent
1. Land	5-078	•31-68	9-018	52*33	13-263	66-17
5. Salt	1-785	11*14	1-882	10*92	2-256	11-25
6. Opium	0-767	4'79	0-958	5-56	1-090	5'44
7. Post Office	0-058	•36	0-071	-42	0-085	•42
8. Stamps	0-067	-42	0-122		0-234	i-t?
9. Customs	0-807	,5-04	.1-159	6-68	1-667	8-32
10. Mint	6-013	-08	0-035	*21	0-057	•29
12. Miscellaneous	7-452	46-49	3-990	23-16	1-392	6-94
Total Avg. Revenue	16-02?	100'	17-235	100*	20*044	loo*
Total Avg. Charges	14-782	92-4	15-490	89-9	19*609	
Average Indian Surplus	1-245		1-745	....	•435	

	Five Years, 1822-3 to 1826-7.		Five Years, 1827-8 to 183J-2.		Five Years, 1832-3101836-7.	
	------ a------					
1. Land .	13-56J	61-83	13-112	60-90	11-942	i7-oo
2. Sayer .				....	0-149	•73
3. Excise.	...				0-004	•02
4. Moturpha					0-019	-09
5. Salt	2-603	11-87	2-590	12'03	2-036	9*72
6, Opium	1-641	7-47	1-747	8*12	1-677	8-00
7. Post Office	0-118	•54	0-124	•58	0-120	•57
8. Stamps	0-329	1-50	0-381	1-77	0-356	1'70
9. Customs	1-663	7-58	1-747	8*12	1-506	7-19
10. Mint	0-035	-<6	0-037	-17	0-066	•3>
11. Tobacco					0-015	•07
12. Miscellaneous.	1-986	9'°5	1-789	8-31	3-059	I4-'60
Total Avg. Revenue	21'942	100*	21-527	100'	20-949	xoo*
Total Avg. Charges	22-184	101*1	20-724	96-3	16-896	io-7
Average Indian Surplus			-803		4-053	
Average Indian De- ficiency......*I*	•242					

TABLE K.—*Continued.*

1	3	S	4	6	6	1
BraochM of'Aevenue.	Five Years, 1837-8 to 1841-2.		Five Years, 1842-3 to 1846-7.		Five Years, 1847-8 to 1851-2.	
	Average ^nntial Revenue.	Ratio of each Branch to Total Revenue	'Average j^nnval Revenue.	Ratio of each Branch to Total Revenue.	Average Annual Revenue.	Ratio of each Branch to Total Revenue.
	Mlns. £	Per Cent.	Mlns. £	Per Cent	Mlns. £	Percent
1. Land	12-380	59·°5_	13-432	55-85	14-947	56-06
2. Sayer	0-725	3'46	0-824	3-,43	1-038	3'89
3. Excise	0-023		0-028	•iz	0-028	•IO
4. Motnrpha	0-103	•49	0-112	•47	0-116'	'43
5. Salt	2-593	»r37	2-798	•J'65	2-438	9'»4
6. Opium	1-547	7-38	2-965	i»'33	3-840	i4'5o
1, Post Office	0-146	•70	0-180	•75	0-189	•70
8. Stamps –	0-424		0-441	1-85	0-470 -	1*75
9. Customs	1-418	6-76	1-449	6-oz	1-439	5'40
10. Mint	0-090	•43	0-092	•38	0-086	•3»
11. Tobacco *...	0-081	•39,	0-089	•37	0-088	•32
12. Miscellaneous	1-434	6-84	1-636	6-80	1-977	7-40
Total Avg. Revenue	10-964	100*	14-046	lOO*	z6'656	lOO*
Total Avg. Charges	19-301	9»'>	22-338	9»'9	24-113	90'5
Average Indian Surplus	1-663		1-708	....	2-543	....
Average Indian De-1 ficiency {				....		....

TABLE L.

Summary of preceding Table {K), ATERAOB Jnnuaf REVENUE <fertW
from all Sources, with PER CENTAOE PROPORTIONS *the Toted of each
Branch, a» raised in the* WHOLE INDIA :—(1) *In the Period of* FOUR
YEARS 1852-3 to *1856-6;* (2) *In the preceding Period of* SESTT YEARS
1792-3 to 1851-2 j (3) *Z» the Aggregate Period of* SIXTT-FOXXR YEARS
1792-3—1866-6.

1	3	3	6	6	1
	Pour Years, 1832-3 to 1855.6. —J		Sixty Years, 1792-3 to 1851-2.		Sixty-Four Years, 1792-3 to1855-6.
Biancites of Revenue.	Average Annwit Revenue.	Ratio of each Branch to Total Revenue.	Average Annual Revenue.	Ratto of each Branch to Total Revenue.	Average Revenue.	Ratio of each Branch to ' Total Revenue.
	Mlns. £	Per Cent.	Mlns. £	Per Cent.	Mina. £	Per Cent.
1. Land	16-183	53'4°'	9-959	53'93	10-349	64'07
2. Sayer .	1-182	4-0S	0-083	•45	0-152	•80
3. Excise.	0-037	•'3	0-081	•44	0.078	•4'
4. Moturpha	0-112	•38	0-100	•54	0-101	•53
5. Salt	2-677	9'17	2-080	n-z6	2-118 - tu	11-07
6. Opium	4-943	16-91	1-449	7-85		8-71
7. Post Office	0-211	•73	O-IOl	•55	0-108	'56
8. Stamps	0-529	rSi 4	0-243	i*3i	0-261	1-36
9. Customs	1-611	S'5»	1-162	6.29	1-190	6'22
10. Mint	0-131	•46	0-045	•14	0-050	'26
11. Tobacco	0-018	*06	0-023	•12	0-022	•II
12. Miscellaneous.........9	1-575	6'39	3-142	J7'ox	3-043	15-90
Total Average Revenue	29*209	100'00	18-468	100'00	'9'«39	100'00
Total Average Charges	27-093	9i'75	17-341.	93'89	17-950	93'78
Average Indian Surplus	2-116	....	1-127		1-189	....
Average Indian Defi-Iciency ....)				....		....

It should be distinctly observed, that according to the definition
of the previous returns, the Surplus or Deficient Revenue in each
year is the Indian Surplus or Deficiency, and is altogether irrespective
of the amount of Home Charges. This is explained in the last four
lines of the following explanatory statement, TABIB M. In this are
given, approximately, the items which, upon an aggregate receipt of

1,224,917,000/. in Sixty-four .Tears, left, after deducting Indian Charges of 1,148,812,000/., an Indian Surplus of 76,105,000/.

This Indian Surplus or Credit has to be Debited (1) with Home Charges during the Sixty-four Tears; (2) with the amount of Debt existing at the beginning of the period, and (3) with the augmentations of the Debt between 1792 and 1856. These, together 130,504,000/., reduced the Indian Surplus to an aggregate Deficiency at 30th April, 1856, of 54,399,000/. nearly, being tlie collective-amount of the then Indian Debt of 50,483,369/., and of 3,915,317/. Home Bond Debt charged on the Revenues of India, as explained at ^eater length in the TABLE F of the second part of this paper.' And in order to bring these figures down to the most recent date, it is only necessary to repeat, that, including the Loan of the present year (1858), the Home Bond Debt does not now exceed 12,000,000/., so that the aggregate Indian Debt charged on the Revenues of India, is at this date (April, 1858) about 64,000,000/.

TABLE M.

SUMMARY *of the Aggregate Amounts of the Branches of* REVENUE *of* INDIA *for the* SIXTY-FOUR YEARS 1792-83 *to* 1855-56, *as per Tables K and L.*

Branches of Revenue.	Amount of Revenue raised.	Period.		BXMABKS,
		Number of Yean.	Dates.	
	Mlns. £			
1. I^nd.........................	66J'3o8	64	i792-3 to 1855-6	This Item of Revenue appears in Bengal, Madras, and Bombay Accounts through-out the period. In Noi^-Western Provinces Accounts from 1834-5. In Punjab Accounts from 1849-50.
2. Bayer & Abkarry	9-729	20	1836-7 to 1855-6	In accounts of Bengal, North-Western Provinces, Madras, and Bombay from 1836-7. Punjab from 1849-50.
3. Excise......!............	4-987	20		In Bengal Accounts exclusively.
4. Moturpha...............	6'455	20		In Madras Accounts exclusively.
5. Salt	■35'532	64	1792-3 to 1855-6	In Bengal Accounts exclusively from 1792-3 to 1812-13. Bengal and Madras, 1813-14 to 1822-3. Bengal, Madras, and Bombay, 1823-4 to 1838 - 9. North -Western Provinces, in addition to the tbreelast-mentioned, 1839-40 to 1855-6. Punjab, *Nil.*

TABLE M.—*Continuedi*

1	2	S	4	6
Branches' of Revenue.	Amount of Revenue raised.	Period.		RKMABKS.
		Number of Years.	Dates.	
	Mlus. £			
6. Opium..............	106-707	64	1792-3 to 1855-6 •	In Bengal Accounts exclusively, 1792-3 to 1819-20. Bengal and Bombay exclusively, 1820-21 to 1855-56,
7. Post Office	6-888	C4	*if tf*	Bengal and Madras, 1792-3 to 1855-6. Bombay, 1813-14 to 1855-6. North-Western Provinces 1835-6 to 1855-6. Punjab, 1849-50 to 1855-6.
8. Stamp Duties	16-697	59	1797-8 to 1855-6	Bengal from 1797-8. Madras from 1813-14. Bombay from 1819-20. North - Western Provinces from 1834-35. Punjab from 1849-50.
9. Customs	76-179	f.4	1792-3 to 1855-6	Bengal, Madras, and Bombay from 1792-3. North-Western Provinces frpm 1834-5. Punjab in 1849-50, and abolished there from 1 Jan., 1850.
10. Mint Dues		64	*tt* •	Bengal from 1792*3. Madras an(f Bombay from 1813-14* North - Western Provinces and Punjab^ *Nil.*
11. Tobacco	••437	18	1836-7 to 1853-4	Madras exclusively from 1836-7 to 1853-4. Then abolished.
12. Miscellaneous .... •	•94'777	64	1792-3 to 1855-6	Same dates as those of Item 1.
P Avenue..............	1274-917			
Dedt, Indian Charges	1148'817	*it*	M 22	
Leaves Indian Surplus *Debit* Home Charges, Debt existing in 1792, and increase of Debt from 1792-3 to1855-6....J	76-ioS •30'504			Calculating the Rupee at *2s.*
Leaves Debt charged! on India at 30th? April, 1856............... J	54'399			(inclusive of Home Bond Debt charged upon the revenues of India. See TABLE F, *ante,)*

As this paperHias already extended to a greater length than was at first contemplated in its preparation, the followisg notes on the several Items of Revenue have been shortened as much as possible.

It will be convenient to refer to each branch of Revenue separately.

(1). LAND-TAX.—So much has already been said respecting this most important source of Revenue, that nothing further need here be repeated beyond the abstracting, from the TABLES K and L, of the figures showing its progress from 1792 to 1856, taking the whole of British India together.

Land Tax.— Whole of India.

Period,	Dates.	Land-Tax. Avenge *Annual* Revenue.	Ratio of Land-Tax to Total Revenue front all Sources.
		£	Per Cent.
5 Years.............	1792- 3 to 1796- 7	4,068,000	50*33
	1797- 8 ,, 1801- 2	4,126,000	42'02
	1802- 3 ,, 1806- 7	4,582,000	3>'99
»»	1807- 8 ,, 1811-12	6,078.000	31'68
	1812-13 ,, 1816-17	9,018,000	5i'33
	1817-18 ,, 1821- 2	13,263,000	66'17
	1822- 3 ,, 1826- 7	13,567,000	61'83
	1827- 8 ,, 1831- 2	13,112,000	60'90
»»	1832- 3 ,, 1836- 7	11,942,000	57'00
	1837- 8 ,, 1841- 2	12,380,000	59'05
M	1842- 3 ,, 1846- 7	13,432,000	55'85
♦» «	1847- 8 ,, 1851- 2	14,947,000	56'06
4 ,, -.............	1852- 3 ft 1855- 6	16,183,000	55'40
fio ,, ...	1792-93 ,, 1851-52	- 9,959,000	53'93
64 ft	1792-93 ,, 1855-56	10,349,000	54'07

This abstract shows, that notwithstanding the reduction of the Assessment, and the greater ease to the people of India which has ensued from their Rents being lowered, the importance 'of the Land-Tax as a branch of Revenue has increased.

Whilst the figures of the average annual Assessment in' each of the several thirteen periods embraced in the above extract are in themselves of use in tracing the progress of the Tax, from the average annual amount of 4,068,000Z. (which it contributed to the Revenue in each of the 5 years 1792-3 to 1796-7), up to the average annual amount of 16,183,000Z. (which it contributed to the Revenue in each of the 4 years 1852-3 to 1866-6), any minute analysis of the per centage increase from one period to another has not been gone into, as the territorial area and extent of population during the separate periods is extremely difficult of ascertainment, and of course is only possible by a very rough approximation. , All that can be accomplished-on this occasion is to present, in a tolerably complete form, one of the set of elements essential to such an enquiry.

On another, and interesting 'topic of investigation, viz.: the proportion of the total Revenue raised from Land-Tax, and from each separate other branch of Eevenne, the preceding TABIES L and M, admit of a condensed and full view being formed. The abstract just given, as regards Land-Tax, will show. that whilst, at the early periods—(take for example the first four, periods from 1792 to 1812)—its proportion of the whole Revenue did not average more than from about 50^ to ji-J per cent.; in the latter periods (taking the last four, from 1837 to 1856), averaged as much as from 59 to 55-J- per cent. ,

As inspection of the tables will readily serve to place in juxta-position similar comparisons of the ratios of the other branches of Revenue, the few notes which space will allow as respects them will be restricted to more general remarks.

(2), SAVER REVENUE.*—Under this head are included *AbTearry, i.e..* Waters (Strong Waters), or Spirit Vendor's licenses, and various ' other miscellaneous branches of Revenue included in the term "Sayer" which appears to have been' given separately in the accounts during the last twenty years only. This branch of Revenue, chiefiy direct in form, but from the nature of its incidence, indirect in its action on the taxed community; has increased from an average of about 149,(XX)Z. per annum between 1832 and 1837, to an average of 1,182,000?. per annum between 1852 and 1856. "

(3). EXCISE.—The date of first appearance of this item separately in the accounts corresponds 'with the preceding.. Its annual average has varied from the sum of 4,QP0?. only in 1836-37, up to 37,000Z. only between 1852 and 1856. We may repeat it only appears iu the Bengal accounts.

(4), MOTUEPHA.—Thia Item has never been included as a sepa-rate bead of revenue in any other than the Madras accounts, and the average receipts from it have varied from 19,000Z. per annum in 1836-7, to 1J2,000Z. per annum in the four years 1852-56.

The Moturpha is of very ancient origin; in fact, coeval with the earliest authentic Hindoo records. It was a species of Income and Property Tax on Profits and on Personal Property and Stock-in-Trade. It was levied upon merchants, manufacturers, weavers, shop-keepers, &c., and upon their trade profits, houses, labour and tools. It may, probably, have been carried to too excessive a minuteness of incidence, so as to render doubtful the pecuniary advantage of its col-lection. This is, however, only a rectifiable condition common to the

---

* The word *Sayer* appears to receive somewhat different etymological definitions io various authorities: but, in the end, they all amount to concurring that it means miscellaneous taxes not included in the great taxes. But this designation is a little inconvenient, as there are some specific sources of Revenue of larger amount than the Sayer Revenue, under the bead of "Miscellaneous," afterwards described, being the number (12) of these Tables and notes. **o**

doctrine of limits as applicable to'fiscal science. It cannot be maintained that, in principle, this tax was unsound. A property and income tax is based upon the broad and general foundation, that the relative wealth, in accumulated and productive property, of the various classes of any community, is the most perfect of available standards for practically keeping up a sufficiently near approach to the proportionality of taxation. It is further justifiable upon the special ground, that by the plan adopted in all great countries where such a tax is in force, a limit is defined of mediocrity of means, or of comparative |)overty, which entitles ,a majority of the people, and the whole of the poorer classes to an exemption from its burden. By this means a virtual contribution from the richer minority in aid of their poorer fellow-subjects,—a voluntary concession of the most equitable and useful nature—is always preserved.

The following is the Clause of the laws of Mdnu under which the ancient Property and Income Tax was levied upon the Hindoos:—

" The Tax on the mercantile class, which in times of prosperity must be only a twelfth part of their crops, and a fiftieth part of their personal profits, may be an eighth of their crops in a time of distress, or a sixth, which is the medium, or even a fourth in great public adversity; but a twentieth of their gains on money, and other moveables, is the highest tax. Serving-men, artizans, and mechanics, must assist by theit labour, but at no time pay taxes."*—(Sir W. Jones.* Translation of Clause 120, Chap. X, of the *Ordinances of Menu,* according to the Gloss of Culluca.)

This tax, the Moturpha, has, it is said, recently (that is, within the last year or two,) been entirely repealed in Madras. We may, therefore, expect not to see its recurrence in the accounts of 1857-8 and future years. It must be assumed that sufficient and weighty reasons for its repeal were apparent to the Government of Madras. But it is a fair open question, whether upon an adequate review of the antecedents of systems of taxation in India, an Income and Property Tax, taking due care that the comparatively poor should be exempted altogether, might not with very great advantage be restored throughout the whole of India.

Take, for instance, the case of a wealthy Zumeendar in Bengal. He has, we will say, an Income of 3,000Z. a-year, derivable, in the proportions of 1,000Z., or one third, from the produce of the land cultivated by his tenants; 1,000Z. or another third, from capital invested in the territorial debt of India; and of 1,000Z., or the remaining third, from interest on capital lent by him on mortgage of real property, or on guaranteed East India Eail\vay Stock. What is his position as a tax payer ?, First, as to his income from Land. We have the authority of the official statements from the East India House, for asserting that the Land-Tax in the Lower Provinces of Bengal, under the Permanent settlement, is on the average about half the amount at which a natural and just amount of rent would be fixed. The Landholder is therefore, as regards the source of thia part of his income, in the same pecuniary position (from an English point of view), as a person having half his property freehold, and the other half on perpetual lease at a rental corresponding to the present natural price or hire of the soil. The Zumeendar is, thus far, exempt from any taxation at all, and he has no Foor Kates nor Tithes to pay.

It may, perhaps, be necessary to notice, in order to show that, in this hypothetical statement, the particulars of his position as to Kent of Land have not been exaggerated, that we might have supposed the whole of the real property from which this 1,000l. per annum is derived, to be exempt from any Land-Tax. For it is well known that large tracts of land in India do not pay one farthing of revenue to the government, as the acts of aU previous rulers have been respected and confirmed in their grants of land as *Enams,* or gifts, *2Iaaffees* and *Lakhurauj,* or lands exempted from revenues, Jagheers or lands held on military or feudal tenure.

Next, as to the second item of his income, viz.: 1,000*l.* from Interest on the territorial debt of India; and as to the remaining third item of 1,000l. income from interest on loans and railway shares it need scarcely be observed that, with the exception of some trifling deed stamps on the Mortgages and transfers, the Kevenue of India takes no part of this Income.

If he smokes Tobacco, the government receive no'lax. If he has a hundred servants, no assessment is made upon him. His carriages and horses are free from any impost.

What then does he contribute, in the shape of direct and indirect taxation, to the Eevenue ? The answer is, that (1) upon the Salt consumed in his house, he contributes to the amount of a few shillings in the year;—(2), that if he indulges in drinking spirituous liquors, the shopkeeper who has to pay for a spirit license or monopoly, charges him a somewhat increased price, so ns to make the tax fall upon him^s a consumer.—And these make up the sum total of his contributions, and instead of some stimulus to exertion being imposed upon him by the government placing a moderately increased burden of taxation at his charge, he is left scot-free ; and the better oflt' he is, the more does he consume of the untaxed commodities of the coxmtry, and the less does he contribute in proportion to his share in its industrial progress, and in its general wealth and resources.

If this be not a disturbance of the equity and proportionality of taxation, we shall have difficulty in discovering what is so. And, if it be such a disturbance, the proposition is established that direct taxation is too much neglected in India.

(5). SXLT-TXX.—This is the only tax universally felt throughout India. There has been much controversy at all times respecting it, and of too complex and lengthy a character to admit of any discussion here. The difficulties attendant on a clear comprehension of its effect on the consumption .and price of Salt, have, however, been much lessened by the recent inquiry instituted by the government of India.

It is not long since an elaborate Report on the Manufacture and Sale of Salt, and on the Tax thereon in British India, was laid before Parliament. This Report, dated Nagpore, 24th May, 1856, is from Mr. George Plowden, Commissioner of Inquiry on Salt. It professes to embrace the whole subject of the supply of Salt for every part ot British India, and to be fitted for a complete text book of reference. The contents, including appendices, take up more than a thousand folio pages.

The following are some of the most important of Mr. Plowden's conclusions (see page 218 of Report) :—

"The Salt Tax is the only tax, direct or indirect, of any description, which labourers, and other poor people, in India, are *obliged* to pay.

" The argument that Salt is the only condiment an Indian labourer consumes with bis food, which is of such a nature that without Salt it would be intolerably insipid, is a mistake of fact.

The Indian labourer, when the facts of his case are ascertained, is proved to be much more fortanate in the fiscal system under which be lives, than the English labourer.

" The whole of the evidence on both sides of the question of monopoly goes to this, that it is impossible to point out any equally prudnctive source of revenue, in India, less objectionable, all things considered, than a moderate Salt Tax.

"The Salt Tax, even at its present high rate in Bengal, is not,' all things considered, ' a heavy and grievous burthen ' to the labouring man, or to any one else living under the protection of the British Government.

" At the same time, the tax is positively too high, even at its present reduced rate, and apart from financial consideratidns, it is very desirable that further reductions should be made.

" If any reduction be made, it should be a reduction of eight annas per maund at one leap."

The space at command absolutely forbids our entering upon ' any review of the Statistics contained in Mr. Plowden'^ very important and voluminous report. A few words are, however, desirable, and upon the conclusions above cited, particularly as to the last two paragraphs upon certain suggested further reductions in the tax. These read as if some explanation were needed to reconcile them with the other conclusions which precede them. Without such explanation, the meaning of the Commissioner would seem to be the advocacy of reduction simply on the general ground (common to most kinds of taxation) that in the hypothetical event of the finances admitting of reduction without detriment to the requirements of the revenue, that course ought to be adopted.

As the progress and proportions of this Tax to the total Eevenue of India at different periods can be easily and conveniently stated, from the tables illustrating this part of our inquiry, I here annex them.

Salt Tax.— Whole of India.

Period.	Bates.	Salt-Tax. Average Revenue.	Ratio to Total Revenue from all Sources.
		£	Per Cent.
5 Years	1792- 3 to 1796- 7	1,207,000	14'95
	1797- 8 ,, 1801- 2	1,188,000	12*10
,,	1802- 3 , 1806- 1	1,589,000	11*09
ft	1807- 8 ■,, 1811-12	1,785,000	11*14
»	1812-13 . 1816-17	1,882,000	10*92
	1817-18 ,, 182V- 2	2,256,000	11'25
»»	1822- 3 ,, 1826- 7	2,603,000	11'87
	1827- 8 ,, 1831- 2	2,590,000	12'OJ
	1832- 3 ,, 1836- 7	2,036,000	9'7z
• >,	1837- 8 ,, 1841- 2	2,593,000	12-3 7-
ft	1842- 3 ,, 1846- 7	2,798,000	11'65
	1847- 8 . 1851- 2	2,438,000	9"i4
4 ..	1852- 3 ,, 1855- 6	2,677,000	
60 ..	1792- 3 ,, 1851- 2	2,080,000	11*26
64 ,,	1792- 3 ,, 1855- 6	2,118,000	11*07

It is satisfactory to observe from these figures that the Salt Tax, in its ratio to the total raised from other branches of Eevenue, has been gradually decreasing.

(6). OPIUM EEVENUE.—The progress of this "branch of the Eevenue of India is shown in the annexed figures:—

Setenu^— FPZofe of India.

Period.	Bates.	Opium. Average Revenue.	Ratio to Total Revenue from all Sources.
		jg	Pec Cent.
5 Years	1792- 3 to 1796- 7	264,000	3*^7
	h 1797- 8 ,, 1801- 2	312,000	3'18
	1802- 3 ,, 1806- 7	579,000	4*04
»»	1807- 8 ,, 1811-12	767,000	4'79
tt	1812-13 ,, 1816-17	958,000	S'56
ft	1817-18 ,, 1821- 2	1,090,000	5'44
»f	1822- 3 ,, 1826- 7	1,641,000	7'47
tt	1827- 8 1831- 2	1,747,000	8*12
•f	1832- 3 ,, 1836- 7	1,677,000	8'00
	1837- 8 ,, 1841- 2	1,547,000	7-38
	1842- 3 ,, 1846- 7	2,965,000	1233
	1847- 8 ,, 1851- 2	3,840,000	^4'5°
4 ,,	1852- 3 ,, 1855- 6	4,943,000	16*91
60 ,,	1792-93 ,, 1851-52	1,449,000	7-85
64 ,,	1792-93 ,,	1,667,000	8'71

'4

It is thus evident that the proportionate importance of the government opium monopoly, as contrasted with the aggregate of other sources of revenue, has increased fivefold in the 64 years, ending in 1856.

No item of Indian Revenue has been so much inveighed against, by foreign as well as by home opponents of the-policy of Great Britain in the East, as the Opium revenue.

It is contended that it is iniquitous to derive a revenue from the sale of a drug prejudicial to the health, and to the physical and moral condition of the Chinese who use it and pay the whole of the tax; but it is a matter of fact that, notwithstanding Imperial edicts and prohibitions, opium is largely cultivated in several parts of China, and the native produce is generally supposed to be nearly equal to the amount of Indian Opium imported. It is ag erroneous to assert that England is amenable to the charge of forcing thia, narcotic upon the two or three millions of Chinese opium smokers, -whose indulgence is supplied by the opium grown in India, as it would be to assert that Erance is amenable to the charge of fostering brandy drinking in the countries which import the produce of Cognac. If India were the only country in which opium could be grown, or if France ■stere the only country in which brandy could be distilled, there might . be some foundation for each of these inductions; but as the contrary to these propositions is the truth, such inductions are fallacious.

The good hide of the opium trade, and the important ends it subserves, are too often quite overlooked by anti-English writers of the " Veuillot de'l'Univers " type.

In the first place, the growth of opium in India gives employment and means of subsistence to thousands of persons; native capital and labour are profitably employed in the transit of the product on land and sea; and European manufactured goods are made cheaper in price, and more within the purchasing power of our Indian fellow-subjects. In the next place, there are the benefits which accrue to China through the great help to commerce aflrarded by the import into China of Indian opium; and besides this, the Chinese are able to devote to cultivation of necessaries of life, that portion of the soil which would be appropriated to the growth of opium, if it wei% not for their preference of the Indian-grown article.

The commercial advantages require more detailed explanation. We are now exporting from the United Kingdom to the East Indies at the rate of about 13,000,000Z. per annum of Home Produce. We indulge in the luxury of Chinese tea, and import Chinese silk for home and foreign consumption, at the rate of (together) about 14,500,000Z. per annum. The Chinese have not yet arrived at a larger development of taste for British manufactured goods than suffices to induce them to import about 2,500,000Z. per annum. We have, therefore, to pay them the difference between 14,500,000*l*., due to them for tea and silk, chiefly, and 2,500,000*l*., due by them for our manufactured goods. We should, therefore, in the present state of the trade, have to remit them 12,000,000*l*. in bullion, were it not that the Celestial Empire has its *wn wants in the shape of opium, and of raw produce of other kinds indigenous to India.

But India is hot a Chinese-tea-drinking, nor Chinese-silk-wearing, country, China, therefore, has to pay India in bullion. At the present rate of the opium trade it would have to pay in thia manner more than 7,000,000*l*. per annum. The United Kingdom exports, as stated, about 13,000,000*l*. of declared annual value to India. On the other hand it has certain balances in its favour due by India, including the sums due by the territorial revenues to cover the charges of the Indian government defrayed in England. To meet these, India would have to remit bullion to England, if it were not for the opium trade.

Through the useful medium of this trade, the 7,000,000*l*. described as due from China to India, for Opium, is "balanced by the 7,000,000*l*. due from India to England. Instead of the costly, circuitous, and hazardous process of China sending 7,000,000*l*. of her bullion to India; India sending 7,000,000*l*. of her bullion to England; and England sending 7,000,000*l*. of her bullion to China; th^se three objects are aU realized by China taking 7,000,000*l*. worth of Opium from India; and thus (1) lightening the Eevenue of British India to the extent of about 4,000,000*l*. per annum, which is<the net receipt from opium; and, (2), ecoAomiZing the use of an aggregate of Twenty-One Millions of bullion, a benefit felt to nearly an equal extent by the three nations concerned; viz., India, China, and the United Kingdom.

(7). POST OFFICE.—The figures of the gross Eevenue from this source may be seen on inspection of the TABLES K and L. From the Year 1839 tS the present time, after the expenses are deducted, a Net deficit has resulted. It requires no more than this to be said, to prove that the Post Office is no burthen on the people of Indi^ even if it were not notorious that the British government following out the successful home plan of penny postage, have extended the benefits of a proportionately lower rate of postage to India.

(.8). STAMP DUTIES.—It is not essential to recapitulate the items of Eevenue from this source, save to remark that they have increased in the annual aggregate from 30,000*l*., in the period 1797-1802, to 529,000*l*. in the period 1852-56,

(9). CUSTOMS.—These are raised from certain descriptions of goods passing the frontiers between British India and the Native States, and by Import and Export Duties. All vexatious iqunicipal

E

eustoms-dutfes or tollage, have long ago- been abolished. The Customs Eeceipts have not increased as much as might be expected with the growth of Indian commerce.. Whether this has arisen from desirable reductions of duty, or chiefly from a laudable wish to promote the cultivation, and export of certain descriptions of raw produce, it is not within the scope of these remarks to enter. The following are the figures showing the progress and retrogression of the gross revenue from this branch:—

Customs Revenue.— Whole of India.

Period.	Dates.	Customa. Average *Annual* Revenue.	Ratio to total Revenue from all Sources.
			Per Cent.
5 Years	1792- 3 to 1796- 7	192,000	2*38
	1797- 8 „ 1801- 2	304,000	3'10
	1802- 3 „ 1806- 7	596,000	4M6
	1807- 8 „ 1811-12	807,000	5'°4
	1812-13 „ 1816-17	1,159,000	6-68
	1817-18 „ 1821-22	1,667,000	8-32
)»	1822- 3 „ 1826- 7	1,663,000	7-58
tf	1827- 8 „ 1831- 2	1,747,000	8-11
ᴓ	1832- 3 „ 1836- 7	1,506,000	7-19
M	1837- 8 „ 1841- 2	1,418,000	6'76
	1842- 3 „ 1846- 7	1,449,000	6'02
	1847- 8 „ 1851- 2	1,439,000	5'4°
4 ..	. 1852- 3 „ 1855- 6	1,611,000	5-Si
60 „	1792- 3 „ 1851- *i"*	1,162,000	6'29
64	1792- 3 „ 1255- 6	1,190,000	6'22

(10). MINT- DUTIES.—This, like the Post Office Eevenue, is sometimes an item of net deficit. In many years, however, the Eeceipts, after deducting all charges, have left a haifdaoine contribution to Eevenue. The item is not of sufficient moment to require recapitulatiod here of all the figures which belong to it, in TABLES K and L. We may restrict ourselves to noticing that the gross Mint Dues have increased from an average of 8,000?. in the period 1792-179Z, to an average of 131,000?. per annum in the period 1852-5G.

(11). TOBACCO.—The Eevenue from Tobacco only existed for eighteen years between 1836-7 to 1853-4, when it was abolished. It does not appear to have been applied to any part of India except the Madras Presidency. The whole gross Sum raised in the 18years was 1,437,000?. The annual amount varied from 76,000?. in the first year of the period, to 63,000?. in 1852-3. The figures for the year of its abolition appear in the accounts of the year 1853-4 at about 9,0002. only, but it may (airly be, assumed that this was only a balance settlement, or for a fractional period of the year prior to the entire cessation of this source of revenue.

If the use of tobacco were likely to prevail extensively in India, it would be difficult to point out any valid objection to the reimposition of a tax upon an article which, by the consent of the leading countries of the world, is one of the .fittest of any for taxation.•

(12). MISOELEANEOVS.—This is the last Item of Eevenue. It comprises annual Tributes paid by native princes under treaty or otherwise, subsidies from similar sources; and certain miscellaneous items (of revenue rather than of taxation) such as pilotage and other charges of the marine and Dock departments; interest on arrears of revenue; judicial receipts; sales of presents from native princes ; &c., &c. The amount of tribute and subsidy from native princes have amounted at various periods to such different sums, that it is obvious much fluctuation has ensued in the amount 'and proportions to total revenue of this particular and special branch. It is desirable to recapitulate the figures.

Miscellaneous Revenue.—Whole of India.

Period.	Dates.	Miscellaneous Revenue. *Annual* Average.	Ratio to Total Revenue from all Sources.
		£	Ver Cent.
5 Years	1792- 3 to 1796- 7	2,315,000	28*64
	1797- 8 „ 1801- 2	3,809.000	38'79
	1802- 3 „ 1801!- 7 •	6,857,000	47'87
	1807- 8 „ 1811-12	7,452,000	46*49
	„ 1812-13 „ 18'16-17	3,990,000	23*16
	1817-18 „ 1821- 2	1,392,000	6*94
	1822- 3 „ 1826- 7	1,986,000	9'05
	1827- 8 „ 1831- 2	1,789,000	8-31
ii	1832- 3 „ 1836- 7	3,059,000	<4'6q
	1837- 8 „ 1841- 2	1,434,000	6*84
	1842- 3 „ 1846- 7	1,636,000	680
	1847- 8 „ 1851- 2	1,977,000	7'4°
	1852- 3 „ 1855- 6	1,575,000	5'39
60 „	1792- 3 „ 1851- 2	3,142,000 ,	17*01
64 „	1792- 3 „ 1855 -6	3,043,000	15*90

It is satisfactory to observe that the Eevenue is less dependent than it used to be upon fluctuations in, this source of income. Whilst on the one side the British government receive Tributes and Subsidies from native states, on the other side it makes allowances to native states.

The following represents, approximatoly, the balance between

E 2*

.payments and receipts ef tbis nature in the year ended SOtli Api'il? 1836:—

* *Ret^pti.*

	£
Tnb.utes from various States *(fiengat^* ------	totjOdo
„ Peislicusb and Sub^dies h(Jfaifre«)	... JXJ,000
„ and Subsidies *(Somiag)*	... 7S,ooo
I'otal....	499»'000

Pagmenfs.

Stipends, Pensions,. Charitable and other Allowances, and Assignments paid out of the Revenues in occordonce with *preaHes or other.engagetaents>^

	£
ling Coorg and'Nagpore, (he Eastern settle-) ments) .... -.............. ✳.....S	£323,CCQ
North-Weef^ Prminces (including allotironees to the) Ex-Royal Family at Delhi, amounting to 333,192/. per annum; andpayments in tbcCis and'Tians-Sutlq States)}	
Punjab, Pensions, Allowances, &c.. ....,.h	10^,000
SPadtae, ft tt	302,000 '
Bombay, tt ⁂ (including Sinde and Sattara)	434,000
Total.........	1,245,000

^usi it appears that against tlie total tribute and subsidies received by the Sriliisb government &om native princes and states, and amounting to about 5OO,OOOZ., there are payments of pensions and allowances made by the British G.pvernmenfc to native princes and states, amounting to about 1,250,000/., leaving a balance against the territorial revenues of British India, of about 750)000/. There is ground, however, for believing, that in consequence of the rebellious conduct of Mie ex-royal family at Delhi, and of other native princes, the net adverse balance upon this Item may now be token at under 500)000/. per annum.

APPEND

TABLE N.

BENGAL COLLECTORATES, AREA, POPULATION, *and* LAND REVENUE, 185fi-66.
*{Including Collectorates geograplicaUg situate in other Presidencies, Imt
comprisedfinanci9iy in the Bengal Accounts).*

Divisions and Districts.	Area. (Approximate.)	Population. 1855.6. (Approximate.)	Land Revenue. 1856.6.
	Sq. Miles.	Millions.	MtHinna. £
BENGAL PROPER.*			
1. Backergunge	3,794	0'734	0'109
2. Bagoorah	2,160	0'900 1	0'022
3. Do. Deputy ......·...............			0'040
4. Burdwan	2,224		0'311
5. Do. Deputy			0'043
6. Chittagong	2,717	I*000	0'080
7. Cooch Behar (see No. 58)			0'007
8. Dacca ....*f.* •	1,960	o*600	0'048
9. Dinagepore	3,820	1'200	0'176
10. Hooghly	2,007	I'S2I	0122
11. Jessore............................	3,512	0'382	0'117
12. Moorshedabad............................	1,856	*•045	0'129
13. Mymensing............................	4,712	•487	0'083
14. Nuddea............................	2,942	0'199	0'120
15. Pumea............................	5,712	i*600	0'100
16. Rajeshahye ●............................	2,084	o'6yi	0'105
17. Rungpore	4,130	2'S5S> {	0'111
18. Do. N. E............................			0'002
19. Sylhet	8,424	0'380	0'043
20. Tipperah	4,850	0'807	0'098
21. Twenty-Four Pergunnahs			0'161
22. Beerboom, Deputy.....................	3,114	1*041	0'076
23. Bullooah, Deputy ....,........	(incld. in 20)	o*600	0'067
24. Calcutta, Deputy........................	(do. in 21)		0'003
25. Furreedpore............................	2,052	o'Sss	0'004
25. Maldab............................	1,288	0'43*	0'027
26. Pubnah............................	2,606	o'600	0'036
27. Maunbhoom............................	(see No. 58)		0'008
28. Darjeeling	(do.)		0'003
	65,964	20'566	2'251

* Under the permanent settlement of 1793.

£ S

TABLE N.—*Continued.*

Diviaions and Districts.	Area. (Approximate.)	Population. 1866-6. (Approximate.)	land Revenue. 1856-6.
	Sq. Miles.	Millions.	UiUions. £
BEBAB PROVINCE.			
30. Behar		2-500	0-154
31. Bhaugulpore		2-000	0-059
32. Dhurrumpore			0-030
33. Patna		1*200	0-119
34. Sanin		1-700	0-182
35. Shahabad		1-600	0-140
36. Tirhoot		2-400	0-166
iT. Monghyr, Deputy		0-800	0-076
38. Hazareebangh			0-006
39. Singbboom		0-200	0-002
40. Suuibulpore		•^74	0-010
41. Lohaduggur			0-005'
	43,465	IZ'674	0-949
ORISSA PROVINCE.			
42. Balasore	1,876	0-556	0-037
43. Cuttack	4,829 }	1-000 j	0-083
44. Pooree			0-044
45. Hidgelee	5,029 }	0-666 j	0-038
46. Midnapore			0-142
28(a).' Mannbboom	(see No. 58)		0-001
47. Puttaspore	(do.)		0-007-
	11,734	2-2XL	0-352
PROVINCES UNDER THE GOVERNOR-GENERAL IN COUNCIL.			
48. Assam	24,531	0-750	0-079
49. Arracau	32,250	0-540	0-071
50. Cacbar	4,000	o-o6o	0-007
51. Tenasserim Provinces	29,168	0-115	0-024 .
52. Pegu and Martaban do	32,250	0-570	0-182
53. Coorg Territory (Madras)	2,116	0-136	0-017
64. Nagpore do	76,432	4-650 '■	0-423
55. Oude' do	25,000	i'000	0-212
56. Eastern Settlements	1,575	0-202	0-095
		12-023	1-110
57. Resumed Lands in Bengal, Behar, and Orissa	(see No. 58)		0-012
58. South-West Frontier and otherl Districts, the Area and Popula* l tion of which are not given in the above list	45,833	4-505	
Total, Bengal Collectorates	394,318	5*'99o	

TABLE O.

NORTH-WESTERN PROVINCES, COLLECTORATES, AREA, POPULATION, *and* LAND REVENUE, 1855-56.

Divisions and Districts.	Area. * (Approximate.)	Population. 1856-6. (Approximate.)	land Bevenue.
	Sq. Miles.	MiUioQB.	MiUioos. £
DELHI DIVISION. «			
1. Bhbttee	3,017	0*113	0-016
2. Delhi	790	0-436	0-046
•3. Goorgaon	1,939	o-66i	0-107
4. Hissar	3,294	0-331	0-045
6. Paneeput	1,270	o'jSp	0-082
6. Rhotuck	1,340	*O'ill*	0-063
	11,650	2-308	0-359
MBEROT DIVISION.			
1. Allyghur	2,152		0-197
8. Bolundahuhur.....................	1,824	0-778	0-107
9. Dbera Dhoon	673	0*033	0-004
10. Meerut................	2,200	1'135	0-169
11. MozufFemuggur	1,646	0-673	0-112
12. Suhamnpore ..	2,162	0-801	0-108
	10,658	*4'5,S4*	0-697
AOBA DIVISION.			
13. Agra...........................	1,865	1*003	0-161
14. Etawah	1,677	0-611	0-127
15. Furruckabad	2,123	1'065	0-135
16. Muttra.......	1,613	0-863	0-168
17. Mynpooree .	2,020	' 0-833	0-127
	9,298	4'174	0-718
ROBILCU\^D DIVISION,			
18. Bareilly	3,119	1'378	0-178
19. Bijnour	1,900	0-696	0-119
20. Budaon...........................	2,402	1*019	0-112
21. Moradabad	2,699	1'138	0-136
22. Shajehanpore	2,308	0-986	0-106
	12,428	5'217	0 651
ALLAHABAD DIVISION.			
23. Allahabad........................	2,788	1-380	0-213
24. Banda	3,010	0'744	0-159
25. Cawnpore........................	2,348	1-175	0-213
26. Futtebpore	1,583	0-680	0-143 .
27. Humeerpore.............................	2,242	0-549	0-114
	11,971	4'528	0-842.

TABLE O.—*Contirtuei.'*

Sirisions and Districts.	Area. (Approximate.)	Population. 1655.6. (Approximate.)	Land Revenue.
	Sq. Miles.	fttiUions.	MiUions. £
BENARES DIVISION.			
28. Azimghurh	2,516		0-150
29. Benares.............................	996	0-852	0-091
30. Ghazeepore	2,181	••596	0-150
31. Goruckpore........................	7.340	3-088	0-212
32. Jaunpore i........................	1,552	1-144	0-125
33. Mirzapore	5,152	1*104 ,	0-084
	19,737	9'437	0-812
	'	-	
SAOGOR DIVISION.			
34. Hoshungabad	1,916	0'^43	0-036
35. Nursingpore......................	501	0'^55 '	0-031
36. Jubbulpore	6,237	0'443	0-052
37. Sangor.............................	1,857	0-306	0-071
	10,511	1'247	0-190
	86,253	31-665	4-269
DISTRICTS.			
38. Ajmere.............................	2,029	0'225	0-037
39. Jliansi	4,405	0-376	(0-067
40. Jaloun			(0-099
41. Kumaon	6,962	o'606	0-021
42. Nimar	302	0-025	0-003
CIS AND TRANS-SVTLEJ.			
43. Umballah..........................	1,832	0-782	0-044
44. Ferozepore	2,545	0-476	0-042
45. Loodiana..........................	1,377	0.-528 ،	0-072
46. Simla			0-002
47. Thanesur..........................	2,3.36	0'497	0-041
48. Hoshyapore.......................	2,204	0-845	0-124
49. Jullunduc.........................	1,381	0*709	0-111
50. Khangra	3,207	0-719	0-067
	28,580	. 5'788	0-730
Total, North-Western Collectorates	114,833	37'453	4.999

TABLE P,

MADRAS COLLECTORATES, AREA, POPULATION, ond LAND REVENUE, 1855-66.

Divisions and Districts.	Area. (Approximate.)	Population. (Approximate.)	Land Revenue.
* 9	Sq. Mites.	Millions.	MiUions. £
1. Ganjam.	*5,758	0'927	0-106
2. Vizagapatam.	4,690	*•25+	0'128
3. Rajabmiuidry	4,501	1*012	0-211
4 Masulipatam.	4,711	0'521	0-112
5. Guntoor	4,752	0'570	0'151
6. Nellore	7,959	1'230	0'154
7. Madras City.	27	0*720	0-006
8. Chingleput	2,717	0-583	0'081
9. Arcot, North Division.	6,580	1'486	0'182
10. „ South Division.	5,020	x*oo6	0'230
11. Tanjore.	3,781	l•6^6	0'447
12. Trichinopoly	2,922	0*709	0'126
13. Madora.	13,545		0-189
14. Tinnevelly	5,482		0'232
15. Malabar	6,050	••5«5	0-183
16. Canara.........	7,132	1'056	0'200
17. Coimbatore	8,151	1'154	0'231
18. Salem	7,499	1'195	0'190
19. Caddapah	13,298	i'45i	0-212
20. Bellary	12,101	1'230	0'196
21 Kumool	3,278	0'273	0-070
Total, Madras Collectorates.	129,974	22'595	3'637

TABLE Q.

BOMBAY COLLECTORATES, AREA, 'POPULATION, *and* LAND REVENUE, 1855-56,

Divisions and Districts.	Area. (Approximate.)	Population. (Approximate.)	Laud Revenue.
	8q. Miles.	UilUoos.	Millioua. £
BOMBAY DISTRICT.			
1 Bombay	18	0'566	0'010
2. Rutnagherry;.	3,964	0'665	0'078
3. Tannah.	5,795	0'875	0'186
4. Sarat	1,629	0'493	0'219
5. Broach	1,319	0'191	0'269
6. Kaira	1,869	0'581	0'241
7. Abmedabad	4,356	0'650	0'188
8. Dbarwar	3,837	0'754	0'191
9. Belgatun	5,405	1'016	0'238
10. Foonab	5,298	0'666	0'120
1'1 Ahmednuggur	9,931	0'996	0'227
12, Sholapoor.	4,991		0'125
13. Candeish	9,311	0'778	0'210
	57,723	9'OI6	2'302
SiNBE DISTRICT.			
14. Kurrachee............................	19,240	0'311	0 061
15, Hydrabad.	26,760	0'703	0'104
16. Sbikarpore	11,532	0'650	0'123
Frontier District	2,147	0'943	
17. Thur and Fackur.	. 3,920	0'051	0'003
	63,599	1'768	0'291
SATTABA FBOVINCB,			
18. Battara......................................	10,222	i'oo6	0'253
Total, Bombay Collectorates.	131,544	11'790	2'846

TABLE R,

PUNJAB COLLECTORATES, AREA, POPULATION, *and* LAND REVENUE, 1855-56.

Divisions and Districts.	Area. (Approximate.)	Population. (Approximate.)	Land Revenue.
	Sq. Miles.	Millions.	Millions.
LAHORE DIVISION.			
1. Umritsur..	2',024	0-884	0-098
2. Goojranwalla	3,752	o'553	0-051
3. Goordaspore................................	1,675	0-787	0-096
4. Lahore..	2,826	0'592.	0-034
5. Sealkote	1,350	0-642	0-077
	11,627	3'458	0-356
JHELUM DIVISION.			
6. Jhelum....................................	5,350	0-429	0-071
7. Rawulpindee	5,996	0'554	0-071
8; Shahpore...........................	3,500	0-262	0-029
9. Gujerat....................................	1,916	0-518	0-054
	16,762	1'763	0-225
LEIA DIVISION.		-	
10. Dhera Gazee Khan........ ■v........	4,000	0'239	0-035
11. Dhera Ismael Khan........	4,123	0-362	0-044
12. Khangurh.............................	1,027	0*212 .	0-044
13. Leia...................................... .т	6,122	0-310	0'-047
	15,272	•1'123	0-170
ItfoouiiAK DIVISION,			
H.'Jhung ..	5,718	0-252	0-020
15. Gqpjaira	4,142	0-308	0-031
16. Mooltan	5,634	0*411	0-058
	15,494	0'971	0-109
PESHAWUE DIVISION,			
17. Haaarah	2,424	0-296	0-016
18. Kohat	2,840	0*101	0-010
19. Peshawar...............................	2,324	0'450	0-068
	7,588	0-847	0-094
Tolal, Punjab Collectorates	66,743	8 162	0-954

TAIBU s.

SoustARY or REsotts.-^WHOhfe *ot ltiDtA.—J^at7s i» preeediufi ^bl«s.-*
(N) M (B)i iW«stv(!.

GoUmtorate Accounts;		Approximate Estimate, as per Tables N to R.				Land Revenue for the Year 183&.S6.	
	Jnchidiug	Area	Populatioih*				
-Vor Presidency ef«*-	' WstricU ond^tintrics under tlie Administration'of—	9%<>nra»(b ' SquttfC Miles.	iCcnI.'d* Total.	*Mittiotts.*	'Per ■Gent, of Total.	*3tittion4.*	PCT iGcnt. of TbtaL
t. Uengat	IGovemor • Generabof V India/ Lt.-Gover* < nor (rf Bengal, Go- 1 Tcrnor *of* Rfadrasi it ffor Coorg only}	394*	47"	52-	39ʻ	4-674	
n. ft.W. Pro-I Tinces'.-J	Lieut.. Governor oH N.W. Provinces ....*i.*	tl5–	'4'	37- '	aS*	d-aop-	
tit. Modros ...	Governor of Madras....	13b-	»5*	23-	*t*«-	3-637	Zl*
tiV. Bombay	Governor of Bombay.;..	131'-	16* ‹	12-	9-	2-846	«7-
V. Punjab.........	Governor-Gen.oflndiu	67-	8-	8-	«•	•954	«-
British States....		837-	too*	132-	100*	17-HO	100*

I-UINTKD UY nAHlllSan AND SONS, ST. MARTINIS bANIS, W.C.